# A Shade
# Written I

My time: 1•4•6•NE**R•1•2•4•9 Neverlandien time

Your time:
1945 Europe. WW2
2000 USA
1920 Europe
1900 Europe

.

# One:

This is my story of how I came to be King of Neverland. I am and will always be Captain Hook King of Neverland. I know that it'll be very hard to destroy the Dark Ones. But I will vanquish the Darkness. And my home will be mine once more.

Questorna Bastosana nuesqi matrononi naxweo wervoin Lightlee .

"May we be strong in the shadow of the Dark Ones, may I get thee back Lightlee."

Part 1
First night:
Once upon a time, there was a man who lived and died. A rich man, a smart man. He was held among the people as the greatest man ever. His name was Gavoth.
This man is not good. He's a greedy piece of filth. This man is not kind. He doesn't care about his fellow men. He'd rather see himself rise above the others, then step on their backs, and look at the world as it moves by. To him other people are nobodies.

Gavoth stared out the enormous window. Gavoth watched as people passed by his mansion.
"They were peasants. Disgusting. They could serve me. And if they don't serve me I could make them die an early death. They will work for me. Oh wait they already do,"
thought Gavoth. He smirked. How happy that made him!
"Mathew! Get in here!" yelled Gavoth. His servant ran into his room and bowed.
"Y...yes, sir? How may I be of help?" asked Mathew. Gavoth noticed that Mathew wouldn't look up at him.
"Look at me when I'm speaking to you. You an insolent fool!" Gavoth sneered down his nose at Matthew. What a worthless fool. Why did he even have this lazy inebriant serve him?
"Yes, sir." Still looking at his feet Gavoth walked towards him but before he could grab the collar of Matthew's shirt a knock came at the door. Gavoth growled in annoyance.
"What!" yelled Gavoth.

A small voice answered, "Sir, the governor wants to see you immediately," said the girl who had opened the door. She was small and worthless, no help at all.

"Get out," growled Gavoth. The girl nodded and tripping over her feet in a hurry to get out she went away. Before she truly left the room she cast a sideward glance at the boy and gave an apologetic smile. She muttered something under her breath and the boy nodded.

"Now what?" muttered Gavoth. The boy stayed silent.

"No silent conversations!" growled Gavoth. The boy looked terrified. Good that will make him easy to control.

Part 2

Second night:

Mathew looked around to be safe. Good no one is there. He opened the chest in his personal rooms. Looking into it Mathew saw the object that laid there. There was a knock on the door. Mathew quickly locked the chest and put it under the floorboards.

"Come in!" he called. The door opened and in came the girl, Aoife. Mathew breathed a sigh of relief. It wasn't the master.

"Were you looking at the secret chest?" Aoife asked. He nodded.

"Well, it's good that I wasn't the master. He would have whipped us good if he found that we were hiding this in your room," said Aoife. Nudging her foot over the floorboards.

You're probably wondering what in the world is in the chest. Well... kind of hard to explain. It is a very rare artifact. Very powerful. Very dangerous. If Gavoth got his filthy hands on the artifact, then the world would be a pile of rubble in no more than ten days. Ya, it's that bad. The name of the artifact is Sialkot.

The Sialkot is basically a skull with intricate carvings. And it's wound with protective spells. If you get past the intricate carvings and survive the burning alive part. Oh wait that is for later but if you did survive the burning part then good for you. It gets worse as we go on. Much, much worse. Do I need to explain the excruciating pain from the spells? No? I thought not. Ok let's continue, it has so much power that if you touch it you'd be burned alive. And again if you didn't listen there are spells weaved in and out of the skull. These are to protect it from being broken. Or continued being stolen by some crazy guy! It is believed that to not be burned alive it needs to be picked up with gloves, that is why it is equipped with thick gloves. They're in the chest. If you didn't notice. Just to let you know.

Is it too tempting to pick up the skull? If not good for you. For those daredevils out there. Uh... I'm worried for your safety. And... life. Don't tell your mother that you are about to do this. She'd freak. Seriously.

Aoife stares at the coals of the dying fire. She heard the steady breathing of Mathew as he slept. He'd been asleep for just a few hours, but Aoife couldn't sleep. She was too wound-up she was thinking.

Never mind I'm not done talking. What was she thinking of? Well, that's a great question. Aoife had been thinking of what would happen if the Master found out that they were hiding a priceless artifact in the floorboards. Scary.

Worse fates have befallen a better woman," thought Aoife. She watched as Mathew stirred in his sleep. She nudged his foot. And he woke up. He looked disheveled. Hair skiwampus. "Is it time?" he asked. Aoife nodded. He sighed and ran a hand through his dirty blond hair. A lock of hair fell across his eye. It was very tempting to move it away and touch his hair. But Aoife didn't know if Mathew would approve of that. So she kept her hands to herself. Mathew was about three years older than her. So he was her elder. He was so handsome. He was a dashing prince.

Part 3

Third night:

Mathew watched as Aoife scratched at the tablet. She had wanted to copy the small spell that had come with the artifact. But she had been working on it for hours and still no progress. She'd only written a few characters of the complex language. The language just looked like little squares with a slanted line through the middle.

Mathew never knew it actually could be a language. Aoife was the language expert. She had been transcribing language for the kings for five years and she had gotten very good. She could just look at the language and know what it means. She said at first she had to use the main codex that helped the transcribers.
Aoife looked up and sighed.
"Finally! I know what it says," whispers Aoife. Mathew nodded.
"What does it say?" asked Mathew.
"It is very complex... it says: "Transire volentibus. Prius necesse est mori. Transiet inferis, ad bypass." Says Aoife. I give Aoife a confused look and she smirks up at me from her place on the floor.

"Or Those who wish to pass. Must die first. Pass underworld, to bypass." Translates Aoife. I nod.
"That makes a little sense, what does the part, 'pass underworld, to bypass?" I ask.
"That's a great question! It means to bypass the underworld you must die. For no mortal can enter the place of the dead," says Aoife as excited as ever. She grinned and looked at the skull.
"Oh thanks that help a lot, English please?" says Mathew. She chuckles and then says, "In the simplest way I can say this is that you need to die. Does it make sense to enter the world of the dead when you're alive?" she shakes her head.
"Nope not really, so I think what it says is that the main puzzle is in the underworld. And you need to die before you go there. Though I know a man who can do us a little favor," says Aoife.
"So is this 'man' going to kill us and then send us to the devil as a little gift? Like, "Here you go two dead mortals!" says Mathew. Aoife smiles and shakes her head and then continues, "No it doesn't mean that he will send us alive to the Underworld." Says Aoife simply. I stare at Aoife.
"But the text says we need to die," Mathew says.
"You're right we do need to die to enter the world of the dead. But remember I don't play by the rules," says Aoife. Mathew smiles as he starts to understand.
"So you're saying we are going to the underworld alive?" asks Mathew.
"Yup we are, are you ready to make the devil annoyed?" asks Aoife. I frown.
"Is your plan to really make the devil mad?" asks Mathew. Aoife laughs.
"That's not our plan... thankfully." Says Aoife.
"Good cause' I'm not ready to make the devil our enemy," says Mathew.
"Well, it's a good time to run... do you have all we need?" asks Aoife. Mathew nods.
"We have nothing, so yes we have everything I have you by my side and then luck also. May we be strong." Says Mathew. He smiles at Aoife and she smiles back.

Part 4
Fourth night:
"Pardon me sir, but your sister is here," said a servant. Gavoth rolled his eyes and told the servant to send her in. She came in with a swirl of dark crimson robes and jewels in her hair. Everyone called her the finest lady of the century. And they were right.
"My dear Gavoth walk with me," said his sister Stella. He walked behind her as she plowed away with her words. Though Gavoth wasn't listening he had other things on his mind. "Gavoth! Are you listening?" yelled Stella. He gave her a blank stare. In return, she rolled her eyes and kept on walking forward.
"Why are you distracted today my dear Gavoth?" asked Stella. Gavoth took a deep breath and continued to walk.
"When I talk to you I expect to be answered!" said Stella.
"Fine if I'm to talk I expect to not be called my dear or any of your despicable pet names dear," said Gavoth with a sneer. She smiles.
"Now there is my original Gavoth. So mean... no mercy..." whispered Stella.
Again Gavoth sneers.
"You know there is only one person I give mercy. And those are the fools of the world, now be quiet I'm thinking." Said Gavoth.

"And you know that your mercy is not even close to being good. You kill anyone that makes you mad." She smiles at that little part and Gavoth growls at her.

"Shut your mouth," growls Gavoth.

"Oh I know you like it, my dear, I know you too well," says Stella.

"And as I was saying, when you're mad you kill them and that is the part I love about you, my dear," whispered Stella. She then smiles up at him.

"You… know… true," whispers Stella slowly.

"And you killed your mother," whispers Stella. Gavoth nods.

"Yes… you're right I did," says Gavoth.

"But now that it's over I have no one to kill," says Gavoth. Then he looks at Stella and smiles an evil grin.

"Who shall I kill next my dearest?" says Gavoth. He then says, "Do you have any ideas?" she smiles and then whispers in his ear. Once she's done he smiles and nods.

"Yes, I think that will do. Thank you, my dear," says Gavoth.

"What would I ever do without you?" asks Gavoth. Stella shrugs her shoulders.

"I have no idea," Stella chuckles. "Now go kill her," says Stella. Gavoth then bows and leaves the courtroom to do his dastardly plans.


Part 5

Fourth night:

Natasha stared out of the window as the world passed by she heard her mother chatting away in the background. But Natasha wasn't listening. She was thinking of her friend Mat. Since the year began her life had gone downhill. First, her mother and father had been divorced. Then she had to move away from her small town. The second she got dumped. Dumped by her beautiful Mat. Gone forever. Her life was in ruins. Natasha sighed.

"Natasha are you all right?" asks her mother. Her mother is a short woman with dark brown hair and blue eyes. Very strange in her family. For everyone in her family had blond hair and blue eyes. And even stranger she had black hair and blue eyes. Natasha nodded.

"It's going to be fine. You'll like the new town we're moving to. I promise," said her mother. Inside she huffed. That promise was fake her mother had never kept her promises. Natasha could tell that her mother knew that she didn't trust her. She could see it hurt her. Good. She turned away and looked out the window. She hears her mother try to explain but eventually she stops. She knows it's useless. Some tears roll down her cheeks and she takes a deep breath and tries to not cry. If she cried her mother would try to fix things. But it wouldn't help. It would just get worse. Much worse than it already is.


Part 6

Sixth night:

"Sir please believe me; I beg of you!" cried the young boy. The young boy was standing outside in the freezing cold pleading with the headmaster.

"You know the rules, boy," said the headmaster. He was staring down his nose at the young boy as he continued to complain.

"But I can't lose my scholarship. I worked so hard for it. Took me three years!" cried the boy. The headmaster shook his head.

"I'm sorry my boy,"

"Now please go back to your home," said he. The young boy's lip started quivering.

"Oh please not the quivering lip, you're grown up now go home, boy!" said the headmaster throwing up his hands. he continued glaring at the boy. The boy hung his head and walked away, trying not to cry.

Now let me tell you the boy's name is Sebastian. His parents sent him to this boarding school. Basically long story short the boy's parents said that if he didn't go to school then they would leave him to die. They had no money so they don't care whether he lives or dies.

Now Sebastian has no place to go. But just wait and see. He might or might not get some help. We go to our dear friend Gamut Slivinski. He's an old librarian. Caring in his old ways but always cautious. We turn to him for help. We also see him sitting by his window watching the world go by.


Gamut watched out his window as the young boy Sebastian slowly walked up the road. Tears streaming down his dirty face. Sebastian calmed the I was the only one who sincerely cared about him. But I bet there were others who cared for the sweet caring young boy. Sebastian knocked on the door and slowly enters the house.

"My dear boy, what is wrong?" I ask. Sebastian shakes his head.

"I don't want to talk about it Gamut, maybe later," says Sebastian.
I shake my head, "No we need to get it over with, what is troubling you?" I ask. Sebastian sighs. He gives a subtle shrug of his shoulders.
"Headmaster Veeter said I can't come anymore since I'm apparently too young. But I'm not!" Sebastian yells the last part. I walk over to him and enfold him in my arms.
"Shush. It's Okay I'll talk to the headmaster. Now get yourself a bite to eat we're going back into town. And I know you hate it but we need to talk to the doctor." I said. So much on his shoulders for such a young boy. Only ten years old, and he's already depressed. Boys of his age should be running around and having fun not doing school. I sigh and walk Sebastian to the small table, where we eat. It's hardly even a table just a piece of a log I found in the woods. I walk to the cupboard and take out the bread and cheese.
To take my mind off the day's events I ask Sebastian, "What did you do today in class?" Sebastian is silent for a few seconds.
Then he says, "We worked on quadratic functions." He mutters. I stare at Sebastian in shock.
"They shouldn't do that quadratic functions are for the older kids, not the younglings," I said.
"I know! That's what I was thinking too. It is so hard. I even put a complaint to the headmaster… that's partly why he said to go home." Said Sebastian hanging his head in shame.
"You shouldn't be ashamed. You did the right thing," I say. Sebastian's face brightens a little bit.
"Thank you Gamut," said Sebastian. I nod.
"My pleasure, I'll talk to the headmaster tomorrow morning. Now go get your stuff, my dear boy." I say. Sebastian nods and walks to his room.


"My boy, you'll have to take Arsenic, with all your problems," the doctor said problems like it was a plague just waiting to spread. I shrink into my chair trying to not be noticed but it was inevitable I was in a doctor's office. The doctor looked down his nose at me like I was a spore. Like I was about to infect him with one-touch. The problem I have is called 'madness' according to the doctor. But it's not true. Well, that's what Gamut said. No matter what he says I'm special. But I don't know what to believe. For my whole life, the doctor's and my teachers have told me I'm worthless but now… I don't know. The doctor jabs the little scope thing at my arm scraping me.
"Sebastian pay attention. This is why you need Arsenic. You hardly pay attention." Said the doctor scolding me. I shake my head.
"I'm listening to you. Also Arsenic is poison. Why do you want to kill me? Is it because of my 'condition'?" I ask. The doctor looks at Gamut like 'can you believe him'? Gamut glares at the doctor and he backs off.
"Where did you find that out my boy?" asks the doctor.
"It's on the bottle sir," I mutter.
The doctor picks up the bottle and says, "Oh… why… your right my boy why didn't I see that?" The doctor laughs nervously like it was a small mistake. But I doubt it, the doctor probably saw that it had that little skull and crossbones thingy. Gamut sighs.
"Sir you shouldn't hurt your patients," he says.
"My god why would I hurt the dear boy. He's like a small virus!" the doctor laughs hysterically at his joke, but Gamut keeps glaring at the doctor. It probably would be a long afternoon.


Today school was a nightmare. The boys kept on teasing me and pushing me around. They knew that I was scared of them but nonetheless they kept on pestering him. Asking me questions like, why are you so dumb? Or do you need a hug, worthless child? These were the most common questions that they'd ask and then they'd burst out laughing and run away. Gamut said it was such a horrible thing to do but I keep telling him that I want to wait the year out. I When I first told Gamut this he was pretty mad. He had wanted to throw something at the boys like a giant rock at their heads. but I told him that was such a bad idea. It took Gamut over a month to get over his anger at the boys at my school. now he just glared at them from a distance. Though I don't believe he's fully recovered. He's probably still raging inside. This is probably why I was sent to him. It's because he has a soft spot for me, though he denies it every time I ask.


Part 7
Seventh night:
Mathew and Aoife walked through the woods. The sun had set hours ago. Even know it was hard to see.

"Aoife, don't you think we should get some rest? We've been going for hours," mutters Mathew.

"Let's put some more distance between Gavoth and his home. I have no interest in having his soldiers finding us in the middle of the woods sleeping and with the artifact. He'd never let us rest, he'd hold it over our heads and make our lives a living hell. Do you really want that?" says Aoife. I shake my head. "Good neither do I. We'll go for about a mile and then we'll find a place to sleep. This I promise," says Aoife. Mathew nods.

"Very well, we will go one more mile. And then we'll find a place to sleep," says Mathew. He smiles at Aoife.

"I know you're tired but we need to put some distance between Gavoth. He can't rule our lives. You know as well as I that he treats his servants terribly. He whips people just because he wants to. And just because he wants to doesn't mean that he holds our fate in his hands," whispers Aoife.

Part 8

Eighth night:

Stella could tell that Gavoth was reveling in his delight. He'd just came back from the murder. His hands covered in dark red blood. I smile at the thought at the sight of him. I chuckle as I remember how the servant girl had run away screaming in terror as Gavoth entered our home. The look of terror on her face was priceless. I'd probably never forget that look. Stella looked up as Gavoth entered the room. His hands were clean and his beard was cleanly trimmed.

"My dear Gavoth you look dashing!" I say standing up.

"May I have this night with you? Dinner?" I inquired. He nods.

"I would love to spend the evening with you, my dear," he says. I smile.

"Finally, he's been gone so much I hardly see him. Tonight will be the night," thought Stella. I head to the door but before I reach the door I feel his arm wrap around my waist. I look up at him as he enfolds me in his embrace. I give him a look and he smiles down at me.

"What's that look for? Is it something I did?" he asks ruefully. I laugh.

"I don't know. Shall we have our dinner?" I ask.

"I bet you're starving after you killed that disgusting girl," I say. He grins.

"You know I'm hungry my dear. And yes let's go eat," says Gavoth he then again puts his arm around my waist and leads me to the door.

Dinner was splendid. A meal of roasted duck and chilled pudding from the cellar. And spicy cider. Gavoth never ceases to amaze me.

Part 9

Ninth night:

I'm sitting quietly near the doors of the Maryinsky. The Maryinsky is the town hall where Tchaikovsky performs his operas. Inside I can hear Tchaikovsky doing his famous opera the Nutcracker. I yearn to go in and listen. To be part of the crowd. But I can't I'm a commoner. A poor child. This is probably as close I can get to actually hearing Nutcracker. I see an older couple walking towards me and I quickly get away from the doors so they don't suspect me eavesdropping. But they don't head to the doors they head straight to me. The older man has a slight smile on his face like he's got a secret to share. I start turning away but the old man calls out for me to stay still.

"Turn around so I can see your face," says the elderly woman. I slowly turn around. When I do I see three tickets in the old man's hands. He notices.

He smiles and asks, "I can see you like Tchaikovsky, my dear boy," I nod. Still not sure what the old man is doing. He smiles again.

"Well I have an extra ticket and I was going to save it for our daughter, but she can't come," says the old man.

"She's got a concert of her own. She's playing the violin," says the old woman.

"Sounds like you're asking me if…" I never get to finish my sentence. For the old man, he grins and says, "Yes! Do you want to come with us and see the Nutcracker?" I stare in shock at the elderly man. I couldn't believe the stock of luck I was having.

"My boy what's your answer. You don't have to accept," says the little old woman. I shake my head. "Sorry, it's just I'm so surprised no one's ever offered this to me before. Are you sure?" I mutter. The old man keeps on smiling. I'm realizing that I'm starting to like him. His easy nature and happy smiles are getting to me.

"Why of course my boy. We don't mind and also we now that Gamut takes care of you. He said that you like Tchaikovsky and said you'd like it," says the woman.

"Can I have your names so I don't have to keep on thinking you as old or elderly man and woman? It's a little tiring," I say. The man laughs a hearty laugh.

"Oh, my dear boy! My name is Valentin and this is my wife Sarah. We now Gamut very well he's a dear friend of ours. And we also knew your parents." Again I stare in shock at them. They seem to never stop surprising me.

"wait you knew my parents? what were they like? Gamut never tells me anything about my parents. I just know they died of the fever," says Sebastian.

"Yes, my dear boy. We knew your parents. Though they didn't die of the fever. they died because they were trying to save your life. And now we see that they did save you from that monster," Valentin's face grows bitter and sad. much different from the joyful expression he had a minute earlier. His wife puts a comforting hand around his shoulders and his expression softens.

"Ah, my dear Sarah. What would I be without you?" says Valentine.

"your parents were the best sword fighters ever. though there was a man named Stanton. he wanted to kill your parents. so he hunted them down. they almost survived, but then something happened. a man your father knew betrayed them and stabbed them both in the heart. then they did their best to save you. it was a long fight. I was there. I was the one who your mother told to take you to Gamut. and watch him from afar. as he grew up. you mother my sister. and my best friend," whispered Sarah. a tear fell down her face. and she buried her face into the shoulder of Valentine. I stare in shock at the news she gave me. they didn't die from the fever as Gamut had said. they had died protecting him to their deaths. he felt an overwhelming sense of gratitude towards Sarah and his parents.

"Thank you for telling me what happened. Though I wonder? Does Gamut know the truth? Or did he lie to me?" whispered Sebastian. Sarah shakes her head.

"No, I told that your parents died of the fever. And that before they died they wanted him to take you into his care. He accepted. And now you've been living your whole life with Gamut. Gamut was a dear friend of my sister and I. I'm glad he took you in," said Sarah.

We spend a few hours watching the Nutcracker. It's so much better than I thought it would be. The music was so beautiful. A few hours later I'm back home and dancing around my room, with the sounds of the Nutcracker in my head. It stays on my head the entire night lulling me into a deep sleep. I dream of people flying across the stage and flipping through the air. Their air and water. Water and light. They're so light. Just flitting across the stage. They're like birds. And then before I know it it's morning. I wake up with Tchaikovsky's Nutcracker still in my dreams and waking thoughts. I go about the daydreaming about one day joining them on stage. Being so light. Being air. Flowing through the air and through the light. I bet all the dancers on the stage now what I'm talking about. The rest of my day is wonderful. I have no worries about the monsters at my school. They hold no fear for me.

Part 10
Tenth night:

I was wrong the monsters at my school do hold fear over me. They control me. They say such cruel things about me. Behind my back and in front of me. It doesn't matter where I am I always hear about it. I've always been tormented by my waking dreams; they walk behind me. They walk in front of me. Always pestering me. Always teasing and joking. Drawing their fingers down my back. And then running. Never do they let me rest. I have no peace. They always with me. outside Making me miserable. Making my life a living hell.

Haven't you ever want to know what will happen to those who torment you in this life next life? I have. I've thought about it every day. Gamut says I shouldn't even think about. My mind shouldn't have worried. I'm too young. I have too much to live for. But is that really true? Do I have a life worth waiting out, Enjoying? Should I be dancing with friends? No. I don't do this. I am Sebastian. I don't know what to live for. I'm raging a war with my mind. And the inner monster within me. And outside of me. There are many mansters in the world. I'm tormented by so many things. They say I'm worthless but never to know about it. I don't know what that means. I'm just a kid of twelve. I. am. Nothing. I. don't. Know. Who. I. am. Those are the words of my life. Right there. Now back there. As I am. I'm back there. The

Monsters of my life say I mean nothing. So I am nothing. I don't exist. My monsters creep around me mocking me. they're in the dark. Constantly laughing. Laughing at me. Scorning me. Figuratively whipping me. They knife me in the back. They are always backbiting. Again I'm no one. I'm nothing. I'm. darkness…

Part 11
Eleventh night:
Natasha looked at the new house. It was horrible. It had the worst color. And the shades looked moldy.
Her mother crowed in delight at the new house. Her mother says, "My dear isn't this the best house you have ever seen? I love this house! We will live in it for the next five years I think!" Natasha shudders and mutters, "This house isn't even suitable for the two of us, can't we move to a place that isn't falling apart?" her mother looked at her and sighs.
"Can you be more positive? We have no money, this is all we can afford my dear," says her mother.
"Don't call me dear. I'm not your dear," says Natasha. Her mother reaches forward to touch her arm but she steps back and says, "Don't touch me! After all, you've done to ruin my life you don't even deserve to be called my mother," Natasha's mother takes a step back in shock. Breathing hard she tries to say sorry but Natasha shakes her head and enters the old house.

Part 12
Twelfth night:
A bullet-shaped knife. It was seven inches long, it hung around Gavoth's wrist swinging back and forth as he worked his sword around hacking at the straw dummy. First at the waist, then at the shoulder. Hacking the straw dummy. He then hacked at the head. It flew off into the distance. Gavoth stood there breathing hard. He saw his sister by him, watching him. He turned towards her and saw that she was holding the rose he had given her earlier that morning. She stared at it longingly. She held it to her nose and smelled the intoxicating scent. A drop of blood ran down her thumb as she pricked her thumb. Before it fell to the ground he ran and caught it. She noticed and looked up at him. A tear rolled down her cheek and he enfolded her in his arms.
"My dear what is wrong?" he whispered. But she didn't answer. She just shook her head. He held her at arm's length and stared into her eyes.
Again he asked Stella, "Stella what is wrong? Answer me," he said. She finally sighed and said, "I don't know."

Part 13
Thirteenth night:
Mathew and Aoife walked through the dense woods. It was still daytime he could see the light falling through the branches. You're This would be the sixth day of traveling non-stop. he was tired and irritable. But he knew he had to keep going.
He heard Aoife whispering the coordinates of the cave they were heading to. They had met an old man and he had given them directions to the cave. But so far it looked as if they were going farther away from the cave. They could see it but once they looked as if they were close to the cave the trail turned abruptly and turned course.
"It seems we aren't close to the cave yet," he said to Aoife. She nodded in agreement and stopped. She sighed. "I don't know why we aren't close yet we've been traveling all morning. Maybe the old man gave wrong directions," she said.
"Well let's try to take a different path. See? The cave is that way," said Mathew. He walked towards the cliff where an opening lay half concealed by the half moon. He could see the cave. The problem was getting there.

Part 14

Fourteenth night:

Stella looked around the corner. She saw the young man sneaking around holding an outrageously large bag. "Wonder what is in it? Is it worth stealing?" thought Stella. The young man turned the corner and she silently followed him. Sadly, the young man turned around and saw her. Well okay, it was sad he would die an early death. Not him seeing her. She was totally fine with slicing his throat. She leaped to him and he jumped back in surprise. "Hey what are…" he didn't get to end his sentence. He fell to the ground lifeless. Smiling she picked up the enormous bag and opened it. A gasp of surprise came out of her as she saw the contents of the bag. Gold and every gem imaginable! Well, today was a success after all. She walked out into the courtyard and saw Gavoth waiting there with a scowl on his face.

"Gavoth is something wrong?" Stella asked Gavoth. He nodded.

"Yup, come with me," he said. She followed him and when they got to the spot he was leading them to she gasped.

"What happened here?" she asked. He sighed and then said, "Attack,"

"By who? The Jeynaks? Or the other families?" asked Stella.

"Jeynaks. They were the ones who attacked. It happened half an hour before you came out," said Gavoth. Stella nodded.

"What shall we do? Give them a little visit?" asked Stella.

"For they know not to attack us. This is our territory," she said this with a sly smile. Gavoth smirked.

"You're right to let's give them a visit. Let's make them fear our names," said Gavoth.

Part 15

Fifteenth night:

The Jeynaks are the third family. There are five families and they hate each other. They have been rivals for centuries. And still, their wish is to slit each other's throats. Even now they are hunting each other down. And killing them violently. Gavoth watches as one of the family's fight. Their names are, Hadrianus and Hartwig. Hadrianus is of the family Aizza. Hartwin is of the family Cyrix. The two young men fought bravely. Hacking each other to pieces. Hartwin had a bloody arm hanging limply at his side, while Hadrianus had his eye stabbed out. He could see.

Pretty obvious who will win huh? The families will probably never stop fighting each other. They hate each other so much. They will do anything to find one of their enemies dead.

Part 16

Sixteenth night:

Natasha looked out of her bedroom window. It was covered with spider webs. She hadn't bothered to clean off the window. Since she didn't plan to stay long. She wanted to leave tonight but it was pretty risky. There were the fairies she had heard about earlier today from the woman in the town. But she wasn't sure who to believe, her mother who had lied to her many times or the woman who she had hardly met.

The house was silent as Natasha crept out of the house. She turned around and jumped in surprise. A young man was sitting on the porch.

"About time Natasha. It's time to lead you to your home," whispered the young man. She tried to take a step back but there was the door. She couldn't go anywhere.

"How do you know my name?" asked Natasha. The young man smiled.

"I've been with you, your whole life, my dear. I've watched you grow up," whispered the young man.

"Doesn't that sound a little creepy?" asked Natasha. The young man seemed to think for a bit and then he said, "Well that depends on how you think about it my dear," changing the subject she said, "OK then what's your name?"

He grinned. "Good question, my name is Peter Pan," he whispered.

"Ya right. You are not Peter Pan. And if you are you're not dressed like him. He's always dressed as a pirate," said Natasha.

"You're right I'm not dressed as him. Because if I did dress as 'him' I would attract the fairies. They'd be here in five seconds. And this you do not want. The fairies may look kind. But they're not. They are murders. They will kill you," whispered Peter. Natasha looked at Peter as if he'd lost his mind.

"You may think I'm losing my mind. But I assure you I'm not. I'm trying to protect you," whispered Peter.

"Hmm… why do I not believe you?" asked Natasha. And then she said, "Oh I know! It's because you're pretending to be a fictitious character from a movie and a book," she continued. Pan sighed.

"Very well. I am nothing. Don't come to me screaming in terror when you see the Dark Ones. Because as you said I'm a fictitious character. I am no one," said Pan. he shrugged his shoulders then, he then stood up and walked into the darkness.

"Wait what are the Dark Ones?" yelled Natasha into the darkness. She waited for an answer but none came. Just silence. The night was utterly silent. As silent as a graveyard.


Part 17
Seventeenth night:
Why didn't the girl believe him? Oh, wait he was a fictional character. He didn't exist. Pan gave a quiet whistle and a dark speck flew through the air.

"What have you called me for?" whispered the dark speck. Pan grinned.

"The girl said I was nothing. That I was a 'fictitious character'" Said, Pan. The dark fleck seemed to make a growling sound.

Pan then said, "Am I fake?"

"No, you were never fake. Now get the girl," whispered the dark speck.

"But as I said already the girl is… insufferable. She said she that she won't come with me. Oh and also she said that she isn't afraid. I thought that this would help," said pan. The dark speck seemed to chuckle and then it said, "Yess that will work perfectly. If you don't get the girl by tonight, I and my friends will get her and then we'll kill you. And you know this wouldn't end well. It would be… a bloody mess. This will be your motivation to get her. Now go get her," said the speck of darkness.

If you're wondering what the dark speck is here's the answer. It's a fairy. None of the fairies are good. The fairies are flesh eaters. And then there are the mermaids. Just imagine them breathing fire. Now imagine them chasing you. Got the image? Oh, and Peter Pan isn't good. He's a liar and a thief. If he wants to do something good it will be at his price and his time.


Chapter 18
Eighteenth night:
Hook stared at the ocean and sighed, what a beautiful morning! The men of his crew seemed to be as happy as him. Except for one man he sat on a barrel of wine and sulked. Hook walked over and kneeled in front of the man. The name of the man was Aster. Aster was the main assassin. He killed for money.

"Aster gee' up. Ye need to do yer job. I am not waiting arooond to have ye sitting on yer butt. Now gee' up," said Hook. Aster glared at Hook and shook his head.

"I not moving from thees spoot," said Aster. Grabbing Aster's shirt Hook hoisted Aster to his feet. That didn't work he plumped back onto the barrel and glared at Hook.

"What's yer problem?" growled Hook.

"Bad day of killing?" he continued.

"Ye know what, let's talk sem place diff," said Hook he grabbed Aster by the arm and hauled him to the boiler room.

When they entered the bowler room Hook closed the door and then turned towards Aster.

"What's yer problem Aster? Was it a bad trade in the killing business?" asked Hook. Aster sighed.

"Yes, the Gal I tried to get saw me and then screamed out. The men came and saw who it was. They came at me. I escaped by the skin of my teeth," said Aster he then said, "Now can I go?" Hook shook his head.

"I've told ye to not run. If We be coming at ye hot ye need tu fight!" said Hook. Aster glared at the captain.

"It's no use. I was caught," said Aster. The captain nodded.

"I know. That's why yer going to do a better job the coming of tomorrow. Because if ye don't you'll get yerself smashed. ye understand me Aster?" asked Captain Hook. Aster nodded and then left the boiler room.

Chapter 19
Nineteenth night:
And of course, the kids at school make my life a recurring nightmare. It happens over and over again. Never stopping. They make my life spin at a dizzying speed. Never stopping. My life rocks before my eyes, making me so dizzy. It seems like I have a constant headache from the boys at school. And you know what? I really don't know what to do with these boys, they can be so cruel, and at the same time so annoying. They seem to always be winning. They think it so funny that I always lose. But Gamut says I need to stand up to them. Two people have only said that to me, Gamut. He's pretty persistent. It would seem Gamut thinks a lot about Honor but who can be sure. I can't, life's a mystery.
Today was surprisingly better. The boys didn't cause me as much grief as usual. Which is surprising since they are very famous in making my life a living hell. Today I made a new friend, her name is Casandra, she's the only person who has been paying attention to me. Casandra, she has a happiness around her that makes me want to forget my troubles. But of course, it's not possible. Casandra, she said she'd be willing to always stand up for me. When she said that I was, well... surprised no one had ever said that to me before, this was pretty new to me having a person other than Gamut on my side.

Chapter 20
Twentieth night:

When I went to my class I'm surprised to see that the person that it's next to me is Casandra's friend Summer. She smiles at me and somehow I get a smile on my face. Summer leans towards me and says, "Casandra told me to come and see how you, are, so here's the question, how are you, Sebastian?" I think for a few seconds and then say, "Well, I could be better without the boys always..." I don't get to finish my sentence because here come the boys. As usual, they surround me and whisper some unknown things about me. They whisper behind their hands and smirk. Then to my surprise Summer stands up and starts to herd of the boys. It was like Summer was a Shepard and they were the wolves. It was the strangest sight I've seen today. Summer then looks back and smiles at me. And since my mind went suddenly blank with shock I couldn't smile back at her. And I wanted to but nope, my brain said,
"You're not smiling today, your gloomy today," Wow not expected brain! Wake up!

Again Casandra comes to sit with me at lunch. Usually, I sit under the big oak tree but lately, she's been joining me and today she brought a few of her friends. Summer, and of course Casandra, Mandy, and Sasha. The girls were so cool I think I actually might join them from now on. They treat me as an equal. Today the conversation around the big oak tree was different. The girls just wanted to speak with me. I really liked it. It was nice to not have the boys being a nightmare. The girls asked me questions like, what do you like to do? Or do you spend a lot of time outside? To the first question, I said, that I liked to read poetry. To this, the girls were surprisingly happy. A few of the girls gave me suggestions of what to read next I think I have a list of thirty books now. To the second question, I said yes. I spent a lot of time outside. Actually, I think most of my life was spent outside. Because I didn't have a lot of friends.

Chapter 21
Twenty-first night:
Today an officer came to the house and told Gamut that it was required of me to serve in the war. Gamut was not happy about this. He kept on yelling at the officer. Eventually, the officer had to have one of his men come and pull Gamut out of the house. I just followed them quietly out of the house. Though I was really surprised at what they did next they tied Gamut to the tree outside and left him there. The officer then said, "I'll be here to pick you up

in the morning buy. Make sure your old man doesn't explode. Or we will be forced to take custody of him," I nodded and he left.

The next morning the officer was at the door as the sun rose in the sky. I tiredly pulled myself out of my bed and got dressed. Gamut gave me a sack of food for the journey and then gave me a hug. While in his embrace he whispered, "come back to the house when they aren't looking, we'll run from there," a stared at Gamut in shock. Is he crazy? That would get both of us killed. But instead of telling him, I shake my head slowly and then walk out the door to where the officer is waiting. The officer looks down at me and gives an encouraging smile. But it doesn't help. I feel like I'm going to my death.

Chapter 22

Twenty-second night:

Stella ran down the street as she chased the filthy thief. She was so close. She just had to get close enough and she'd be able to through the poisoned knife. She had been coating her blades in poison when she heard the thief enter. The young man didn't expect her to be in the room right next to the front common room.

When she heard the thief enter she quietly slipped into the secret passage and followed the passage to the slit in the wall that allowed her to peek at the intruder. He was a young boy about the age of fifteen. Dark blond hair surprisingly pleasant features. It would be a shame to kill him so soon. Stella then had an idea. She could just put him to sleep and then find out more. Maybe make his life a living hell. She smiled at the thought. She reached into her pack and replaced the poison coated knife with the sleeper knife.

A few minutes later she had the boy over her shoulder. She ran through the quiet streets. All was silent all was perfect. For now, the streets would be quiet. But soon they would explode with life. It would be the perfect time to do her tricks. Cause some misery.

Chapter 23

Twenty-third night:

Stella stared at the young man, from the shadow's, as he came to wakefulness. He opened his eyes and looked around. He was confused... good, that will make it easier for Stella to interrogate him. The man tried to get up but he couldn't. Because of course he was tied to the metal post that stood out of the ground.

"What am I doing here?" muttered the young man. Stella stood up and walked into the light. She smiled down at him and then said, "I'm glad you awake Maddox, it's about time," the young man looked at Stella and said, "How do you know my name?"

"I know many things, but what I want to know is why did you steal from me?" she said coldly. Maddox sighed and shook his head.

"Probably know that I'll never give you this information lady," said Maddox. Stella smiled and then held the object she was holding. The man started in surprise. He looked at him and then sighed.

"Okay lady how did you get my satchel?" asked Maddox.

"Hmm... should I open the satchel and see what is in it?" whispered Stella. Maddox shook his head. His face forming an expression of panic.

"No! Please don't. Do you even know what's in the satchel?" yelled Maddox. Stella grimaced. He noticed and smiled and continued to yell she sighed and grabbed the dagger next to her. Boys were such idiots. She then hurled the dagger at his leg, and he collapsed and didn't move.

An hour later he came too and looked around. "Did you have to hurl that dagger at me?" asked Maddox. She smiled and walked towards him. "Now tell me what's in the satchel?" said Stella. Maddox shook his head and said, "I'll never tell you as long as I live!"

"Very well then you will be in pain all your life. You'll spend your days down here, cold, no food, all alone," said Stella. She then walked out of the room and up the stairs. She shook her head. Maddox was impossible.

Chapter 24

Twenty-fourth night:

Gavoth sat and listen to his sister describe the events of the week. He'd been gone on an errand and hadn't had time to talk to her. She described the incident with the thief, Maddox. He shook his head in annoyance.

"Wonder why he didn't give in? he has already had the sleep dagger thrown at him. I'm surprised that he hasn't given in yet. As you said earlier, he's impossible." Said Gavoth. He seemed to think for a bit and then he said, "Would you allow me to do my tricks on him?" he said this with an evil glint in his eye. Stella understood what he meant, she chuckled and nodded.

"Of course you may. That is a brilliant idea. This is why my brother you're here!" said Stella laughing.

"Very well show him to me. I'll do my best to torture him. Make him wish he never was born!" said Gavoth.

"follow me, brother. I'll show you the thief," said Stella. She led Gavoth down some stairs and through some dark halls. She finally arrived at an iron door. She grabbed a key from her pocket and inserted it into the door. A soft click came from the door and it quietly opened on well-oiled hinges.

"He's in here, follow me," said Stella. The young man was slumped against a metal post that stood out of the ground. He slowly entered the room and waited in the
shadows. Gavoth waited for the young man to wake. When he did he'd be sorry.

Chapter 25

Twenty-fifth night:

Gavoth saw the young man stir in his sleep. He slowly opened one eye. He opened both eyes and looked around sleepily.

"Where are you? I know you're in here." Said the young man now fully awake.

"You witch come out and face me!" yelled the young man. Gavoth spoke from the shadows. "You're right she is in here but she doesn't want to hear from you, boy," said Gavoth. He then stepped out of the shadows. It was clear that the young man recognized him. He was plainly terrified of him.

"What are you doing here master Gavoth?" the young man's voice shook a little. Good, he should be scared of him. He gave the young man a wicked smile and stepped towards him. The young man coward at the sight of Gavoth.

"Please don't hurt me," whispered the young man.

"What's your name boy?" asked Gavoth towering over him like a mountain.

"Maddox sir. Now that I have told you my name may I please leave?" asked Maddox. Gavoth tilted his head back and looked down on Maddox.

"Hmm... I don't know. You called my sister a witch. Maybe I'll hang you from your toes, then cut a hole at the top of your head so all the blood drains out. You'll slowly turn into a dried corpse," said Gavoth. He again smiled. Maddox paled.

"Please don't do this!" the young man was practically yelling.

"I didn't know she was your sister! I'm sorry. Give me mercy!" yelled the boy frantically. Gavoth scoffed.

"Mercy!? Why should I give you mercy, you're a filthy piece of crap!" yelled Gavoth. Maddox started to shake.

"Oh, great I made you cry! Shut your mouth!" growled Gavoth.

"Now tell me why did you steal from me and my sister!?" yelled Gavoth.

"Because I was asked to. The king he ordered me to steal from you," cried the boy. Gavoth smiled in satisfaction.

"Okay, that's all go live your pitiful life in this cave. But since you stole from me and my sister you're not coming out of here alive," said Gavoth straightening his shirt. He turned around and walked out. He could hear the young man crying in terror. He heard Stella close the door and run to catch up to him.

"That was fantastic Gavoth!" cried Stella.

Chapter 26

Twenty-sixth night:

Mathew and Aoife trudged through the muddy swamp. Flies flying over their heads. Frogs croaking in the swamp. It was so humid. So hot. Sweat rolled off they're faced like individual waterfalls. Mathew breathing hard asked, "where, in the world are we?" Aoife shook her head.

"I have no clue I'm pretty sure we passed through this swamp already," said Aoife. Mathew nodded in agreement.

"You need assistance my dear children?" asked a voice in the fog. Mathew and Aoife stop in surprise and look around.

"Where are you?" call Mathew and Aoife at the same time. The voice chuckles.

"Follow me," the voice purred. They take a few steps and then they hear something else.

"Wait! Don't follow her. She's the evil witch of the swamp! Don't trust her!" called the second voice.

"The voices might both be the witch. Or they could both be separate people but both evil. I don't think we should trust them," said Mathew.

"Smart boy. You are right I am just one person. But I'm also very cunning. What will you do about that?" said the voice. The voice kept coming closer and finally, a figure stepped out of the fog. It was a young woman. Very beautiful. Mathew stared at her in shock. Aoife nudged him in the ribs and he looked closer. Something was wrong. Then finally Mathew figured it out. She had blood red eyes that would follow him and Aoife everywhere.

"You are evil aren't you?" asked Aoife. The young woman nodded and smiled her teeth were filed to tiny points. Aoife and Mathew take a step in surprise.

"What the?" whispered Mathew.

"Shark teeth?" asked Aoife. The witch shook her head.

"Neither," said the young woman.

"Then what?" asked Mathew. She shook her head.

"Not yet my dear. You haven't proved yourself. And to do that you need to go to the good witch at the very end of the swamp you have been walking in for weeks," said the witch. Mathew and Aoife stare at the witch in shock.

"We've been here for weeks? How many?" asked Aoife in a panicked tone. The witch smiles and nods.

"Yes," she paused for a moment and then said, "You've been here for three weeks," said the witch.

"Let me introduce myself to you. I'm the witch Oleander," said Oleander.

Chapter 27

Twenty-seventh night:

Hook walked through the dense forest. Following him were his boys, they were the between the ages of five and sixteen. The youngest, Mika, followed at Hook's heals. There was a content smile on little Mika's face as he followed in tow.

"Hook where are we going?" asked Mika. Hook smiled.

"We're going somewhere special my dear boy," said Hook. The boy took an excited breath. And then skipped forward.

"What's the special place?" asked Mika.

"Just wait and see. Remember it's a surprise!" said Hook. He smiled down at Mika. Mika then held his arms up and Hook swept him up into his arms. Mika giggled, "Up Hook! Up!" cried Mika. A smile spread across his face and Hook chuckled. Concentrating Hook lifted off the ground and flew into the air. It was much harder to fly than Pan. Pan could do it with no thought. He could just jump into the air and be flying while Hook had to concentrate. Mika giggled with excitement.

"More! More! Hook go up!" called Mika. Hook laughed with delight. Soaring through the air Hook alighted in a tree. Surveying the land, he spotted the Dark Ones running towards him. Jumping down from the tree and running towards his boys he started to scream.

"Run! Dark Ones ahead! Move now!" he bellowed. The boys scattered in panic and ran through the forest. He could hear the piercing screams of the Dark Ones as they flew towards them. Kneeling down to speak with Mika, Hook said, "Now you need to run as your little feet can. Do you understand?" Mika nodded. Fear flashed in his eyes. Putting a hand on Mika's shoulder Hook said, "It will be alright. You just need to run. Run fast, my dear boy! I'll meet you back at the Castle," again Mika nodded. Then he turned around and dashed into the dense forest. Praying that his boys would be alright he grabbed the Iron and silver sword at his side. It had been a gift from the Queen of the Elves many ages ago. She told him it was only to be used to protect the innocent, the helpless, the homeless. The children of the world. If he used it for other purposes he'd lose his powers and the powers to fly. He'd be banished from Neverland.

"You are to be the guardian of Neverland. Protect it with your life my dear Hook," the Queen had said. Pulling it out of its sheath he leaped off the ledge he'd been standing on and flew off into the air. Spotting the Dark Ones, he quietly flew towards the danger. But it was too soon the Dark Ones spotted Hook flying through the air. The one that looked like the leader grinned up at Hook and then said in a rumbling voice, "Oh if it isn't our friend Hook. It's very good to see you, captain," said the first Dark One.

"You know I'll never serve you and your foul master. Now go back to your dark pit from where you came from," called Hook. He was so tired of the Dark Ones coming every three days and asking him to join them. They knew well enough that he'd rather die than serve their dark lord.

"What are you going to do to us boy?" said the second Dark One. Hook smiled, but he said nothing. He seemed to be waiting for something. The third Dark One scowled and leaped off the ground trying to catch Hook but he was too high.

Hook grinned, "Too far up aren't I?" Hook gave the Dark One a pouting face and the leaped again into the air.

"Catch me if you can boys!" called Hook with delight. The three Dark ones shook their heads in annoyance. Leaping up into the air they spread giant wings and took off after Hook. Being ten times larger than Hook they had to beat their wings harder. While Hook just flitted from branch to branch. The Dark Ones growled in frustration. The first Dark One dived to the ground. The others followed him. Hook looked back and grinned.

"Got tired boys? I could keep this all day!" Hook laughed.

"What are you going to do about this?" called Hook from the top of a tree.

"We're going to wait here for you until you come down," called the second Dark One.

"You know that's not going to happen boys. I'll just stay up here until you leave. Or get tired," called Hook.

"And while I'm up here let's talk business. Where is Pan?" asked Hook.

"We can't and we won't tell you Hook. He is our 'friend'," said the third Dark One. Hook scoffed.

"He's not your friend. He's your servant. He serves you. He serves the incarnate of the devil," hook called this down the tree he was alighted atop. The Dark Ones leaped into the air in anger. But before they were a few feet off the ground Hook grabbed three small daggers from his belt and hurled them at their wings. There was a screech of pain and the Dark ones fell to the ground. Dark blood bled out of their wings and they looked up at Hook with hatred in their eyes.

"You will regret that you ever did that, boy. We'll come and kill you sooner or later. We will get you!" screamed the Dark Ones. They then put their heads together and muttered something evil and cruel. Hook stood patiently at the top of the tree. Then all of a sudden the Dark Ones lifted their heads and yelled one of their dark spells. Hook had just enough time to dodge out of the way. The dark spell hurtled towards the tree next to him. When it hit the tree exploded and splinters of wood flew in every direction. When the wood reached the ground it's decayed in five seconds. And the ground around the moldy pieces of wood was chard black. At the touch of a wisp of wind, the grass disintegrated into ash. Hook muttered a cry of surprise.

"That's more like it boys! Bravo!" Laughed Hook.

"Let's see what else you can do! Let's is what you've got boys!" called down Hook.

"We have done more than enough Hook, now leave us!" called the second Dark One.

"How about you leave me, for this is my territory! Your territory is twenty miles south of here! Now get out!" yelled Hook. The Dark Ones shook their heads, think and in a flash of blinding light, they were gone.

Chapter 28

Twenty-eighth night:

Pan watched as Hook jumped from tree to tree. Taunting the Dark Ones. He'd been doing it for ten minutes. It was the second time he had done this. The first time he'd done it was a lot like this situation. But the first one is also different. The Dark Ones had come to Pan and delayed the events of what had happened. He'd laughed. He had said, "I'll come the next time he taunts you, but seriously this is quite funny!" he then had burst into laughter. The Dark Ones had then left in a flash of light. Today was the first time he'd see them for weeks. Well, today should be interesting.

The Dark Ones were saying, "We will kill you sooner or later," Pan tried to not laugh as the Dark Ones tried to lift to the air. They were hopeless. Pan actually started to feel sorry for the Dark Ones. Then he corrected himself. He couldn't afford to feel sorry for them they were much powerful than he. Pan shook his head; the Dark Ones could kill him with a flick of their claw-like fingers.

"Is that the best you can do Boys?" called Hook from a tree. He was grinning down at the Dark Ones.

"You will die Hook!" screamed one of the Dark Ones.

"die me? What a preposterous idea" asked Hook incredulously.

"I'm pretty sure that it's you who will die," called Hook. The Dark Ones sneered up at Hook. Hook shook his head in disappointment. And he said the obvious.

"You boys are helpless! How are you ever going to kill me? You're way down there on the ground. You can't even fly! Then there's me who's way up here," Hook paused for a second and then he grinned. "What are you going to do about that?" asked Hook from an enormous tree.

"We will wait patiently Hook. And then when the time comes we will kill you! We will end your life," then the Dark Ones cackled.

"We won't kill you quickly! Oh no! We will make your death very slow. And very painful!" yelled the Dark Ones.

"You will regret that you were ever born to this world Hook! You will die! We promise you that!" they yelled in unison then they burst into flames.

Part 29

Twenty-ninth night:

Hmmf, showoffs! Pan started to turn around when Hook called out, "I know that you're here Pan don't try to fake it, come out now!" called Hook from a tree. Oops, time to run. He took off at a sprint and before he could reach the end of the demolished forest Hook flew in front of him and grabbed him by the collar.

"You're not going anywhere Pan you need to answer for all that you've done. You've already killed some of my boys. That's murder," said Hook simply. Pan shook his head. He knew he was lying but he didn't want to deal with Hook right now.

"Let me go, Hook," said Pan with a warning tone in his voice. But Hook shook his head.

"Oh I'm not done with you, you killed fifteen of my boys," said Hook. He then grinned.

"Should I take you to the queen?" asked Hook ruefully. Pan paled considerably. He started to shake his head but Pan glared at him.

"You need some time to think of what you've done," said Hook.

"Are you kidding me? I didn't do anything! Your boys rampaged through my castle trying to look for something!" he glared at Hook then his expression changed. Changed to suspicion. "Why did you send your boys to my home?" asked Pan. Hook smiled.

"That's classified information. You don't get to find out why I sent the boys to your home until you go and have your time in the salt mines," said Hook.

"In the salt mines? I'm not a criminal!" yelled Pan.

"Oh, I think you are. You tried to kill the queen three times. But that's pretty weird huh? You used to love her, didn't you? Then you killed my boys. That definitely deserves some time in the salt mines, I've heard that you've spent your share at the mines, Pan. What was that for?" said a voice. Pan turned around and saw the elf woman. She glared down at him like he was trash.

"What?!" yelled Pan at her. She smirked and looked at Hook.

"What shall we do to this infidel?" asked the elf woman.

"As I said we'll send him to the salt mines for what he did. Though the part of trying to kill the Queen five times was an unexpected part. For that he will spend an extra five years in the mines," said Hook he looked down at Pan. Earlier he had tied Pan to a tree. He was well-known for his very tight knots. Pan had tried to get out of them but he only succeeded in cutting his wrists. Pan glared at Hook he was again reduced to a nobody. To a slave. Hook would pay for this sooner or later.

"Are you rested up to use both of our magic to send Pan to the mines with a formal invitation to the mining leader?" asked Hook. The elf woman nodded.

"Of course I'm ready. I've been wanting to do this for centuries. He caused my people much pain," she said. She then grabbed Hook by the wrist and they both started to glow. Hook grabbed Pan by the forearm. A searing pain went through his forearm, making him wince. Then in five seconds, they were in a depthless void. They were at the entrance of the mines before Pan could blink. The funny part was the magic had also brought the tree Pan was tied too. He chuckled. That was a bad idea, the elf woman kicked Pan in the ribs. And he gasped for breath.

"Be silent you fool. You will make no sound. For remember you are nobody. You are a slave which means you will talk to nobody and look at nobody!" growled the elf woman.

"Do you understand fool?" asked the elf woman. Pan glared at the elf woman. Once again he was reduced to nothing. Again she kicked him in the ribs.

"I asked you a question fool. I expect you to answer!" yelled the elf woman. Reluctantly Pan nodded. She smiled in satisfaction.

"Very good, if you keep this up you will be treated fairly. But if you fail to act like this you will be whipped for being foolish," whispered the elf woman in Pan's ear. He nodded. He understood. A tall man walked towards them, he was clearly the leader of the mines.

"Ah Hook, it's good to see you again! I see you've brought the little pest," said the man. The man didn't even have the guts to refer me to my real name. how low. He then noticed the elf woman.

"Oh forgive me for not noticing you. How can I be of service your majesty?" said the man bowing. 'your majesty'? when had that happened? The elf woman smiled.

"It is good to see you Patonius," said the elf woman. Patonius smiles relieved.

"Thank you, your highness, should I refer to your name?" asked Patonius. She nodded.

"Very well I except Ava," Patonius smiles and then looks my direction.

"Hmm if it isn't Pan. Come back to us?" asked Patonius. I nodded.

"Well must have been pretty bad," laughed Patonius. The others laughed with him.

"Well come this way I'll show you where he will be staying," said Patonius. He then led Hook and Ava inside the mine sleep stations. Patonius pointed to a very small room.

"This is where he'll be staying he'll get up at six o' clock every morning and mine until dusk. There's a break for breakfast after first shift then he'll go back to work in the mines then there's the break for lunch. After lunch, he'll have a rest period. After that, he'll work until dusk. This will repeat for however long he's to stay with us," said Patonius.

"How long will he be staying with us Hook?" asked Patonius.

"Well, I just found out that Pan tried and failed to assassinate the elf Queen five times. So that will be forty months and then there's the part about killing some of my boys. He claimed they rampaged through his 'castle' but they weren't they were only looking for the human girl that he took from Earth. So that will be an extra ten months. Adding them up that will be…" Hook seemed to think for a bit and then he said, "It will be a total of about three years. So the total years he will work in the mines is twenty years," said Hook. I visibly pale. Patonius notices.

"That's a lot of mine work ain't it?" asks Patonius. I nod.

"I shouldn't deserve this," I mutter.

"You do deserve this Pan. It's for the best," said Hook.

"The slave shouldn't speak to the higher race," says Patonius. He slaps me in the face and I fall back. Glaring up at him I sit back up.

"For the best? The best?!" I yell.

"Be careful of what you say. For now, you are a slave and every word you say will get you hurt," said Hook.

"Why should you care if I get hurt? You sent me here!" I yell. Again Patonius slaps me. And then I make my first mistake. I spit at Patonius. In return he kicks me so hard I feel a rib crack I curl in a ball on the ground groaning.

"Make wiser decisions Pan," says Hook. He then turns around and walks away. Leaving me here with the elf princess and Patonius. My owner. I hate the sound of that word. Again I'm reminded that I'm worthless just a slave. Patonius grabbed my arm and drags me to my sleeping place. He dumps me in the straw.

"Be wiser next time boy," says Patonius.

"I might not be so lucky next time if I continue to stay here," muttered Pan. in return of saying this I get a kick in the ribs. it hurts so much. it brings tears to my eyes. I glare at Patonius. and he smirks.

"I think we might've taught you some humility, ay Pan?" says Patonius. He leans down to my level and spits in my face. his breath smells of tobacco and rotting fish. I recoiled at the smell and Patonius smiles. His teeth are black tombstones. And I cringe. what man lets himself smile at others when his smile is so gruesome? But maybe he doesn't care. I pretend that it doesn't bother me. but inside my guts are twisting in anger. I am not worthless! This I yell in my mind. I sure hope Patonius hears me. Cause' my yell is deafening. Again I am brought to my knees and made a slave someone of no importance. Why did I have to provoke Hook? How could I have been so stupid? I am reminded of what my mother had told me long ago: "Don't say things you'll regret. it can get you into deep trouble. Know that I love you, my son." That was his father's voice. Why did that have to come to mind? It was too painful. It was a reminder of his previous life on earth. When he wasn't immortal. Pan gasped, how had he remembered that? It had been two hundred years since he had lived on earth. He barely remembered his life on earth. Had it been a good life? Then Pan saw younger boys beating up a young boy. then he realized that the young boy was himself. Then the image was gone. Where did that come from? Had he been in Neverland too long that he had forgotten his previous life? Or had he purposefully forgotten it because it was too painful? Was it painful? He couldn't remember. This left Pan to wonder what had made himself to wipe his memories of an earth he had lived on.

Chapter 30
Thirtieth night:
Natasha stared around at the unfamiliar scenery. Where was she? Looked like nothing of her home in Oklahoma. Again where was she? She heard a rustle in the bushes and she whirled around and a small boy walked out of the bushes and glared at her. Could this day get any weirder?

"What ye doing lass? Ye don't belong here lass, get out of this land before he finds you! Go know!" the boy's voice is frantic with terror. What is he talking about? She gave him a puzzled look.

"What in the world are you talking about kid? I'm in the U.S or somewhere in Oklahoma," said Natasha. The young boy shook his head.

"Ye definitely not in Oklahoma lass you need to run!" said the boy. Grabbing at the small dagger at his side he walked towards her with a hard glint in his eyes.

"Ye need to run lass," he muttered. Continuing to walk towards him with the small dagger.

"Whoa chill kid I'm just lost," said Natasha nervously.

"That's even worse lass," said the boy.

"Ok kid I'm just going to leave, forget I was even here," said Natasha. She started to head towards the big forest but the boy yelled at her, "Not that way miss that wood is evil ye need to run," the boy started to chase after her.

"Get away from me you creep!" cried Natasha.

"I'm trying to save yer' life lass," yelled the boy.

"Go find someone else so save but not me, filthy creep!" yelled Natasha.

"Fine, I will save someone else! But let me warn you, you'll find more dangerous creatures here than you will from where you come from, don't cry out in terror when you meet the Dark Ones or the Sisters!" called the boy from behind her.

"Wait for Dark Ones? The Sisters? Who are they?" said Natasha suddenly stopping the young boy ran straight into her in surprise. Nocking both of them over.

"You've heard about them before? Who told you?" asked the boy. They both got up and brushed themselves up.

"Yes, a boy not much older than you named… oh what was his name?" said Natasha. The boy had gone pale.

"You meet Pan. What did he say to you?" asked the boy.

"I can't remember what he said to me. Is that bad?" asked Natasha. The boy nodded.

"You're doomed," he said simply.

"So to answer your question the Dark Ones are basically evil elves. That want to take control of my world and yours. Then there's The Sisters. They are mermaids that suck out your life force. And they breathe fire. Any more questions?" asked the boy. Natasha stared at the young boy in shock. How could this be possible?

"Am I even in my world?" asked Natasha. The boy shook his head.

"Nope. And I'm guessing that I should tell you my name. I'm William. The second command to Hook," said William.

"I thought that Captain Hook was evil and Pan was good," said Natasha.

"It's twisted. Hook is good and Pan is plain crazy. He's evil, a psychopath. Don't trust him whatever you do," said William.

"Though I guess since you're already in Neverland I should take you to the Cap'n. Follow me, lass," in shock I followed him through a dark path in the woods.

"Don't stray from the path or you'll get killed by who knows what. Even I who has been here most of my life doesn't know what is in this wood," said William as he headed in a general direction.

"Where are we going?" asked Natasha. William smiled.

"To the Cap'n," said William.

Chapter 31

Thirty-first night:

The bombs shook the ground as they tumbled from the sky. It was a nightmare. Sebastian was terrified. The smell of blood and smoke was too much he tries not to gag. A man screams as shrapnel cuts through him. A war zone was not a good place for a boy of fifteen. Another man screamed as he got shot in the throat. Sebastian saw the man fall to the ground lifeless. No one could help him now. He was going to die soon enough. The thunder of drones as they flew over his head made Sebastian flinch. His newly found friend grabbed him around the waist and pulled him to the ground as a volley of bullets flew overhead. He stared in shock around him. He'd never imagine that the war zone could ever be like this. So bloody. So loud. It was hot and cold at the same time. The scenery was pandemonium. Hellfire. A nightmare. Sebastian looked around to see if he could spot his friend. He'd just been saved. Was it his friend or someone else in the barracks? Or was it someone in his troop? He couldn't tell. He heard yelling. That didn't matter everyone was always yelling in the war zone. Then suddenly someone pushed him over.

"Get down!" a voice hissed. He tried to look into the person's face but the person wouldn't let him.

"Who are you?" rasped Sebastian. His face hadn't been used, and with the smoke, it made it worse.

"Your friend," said the voice.

"What's your name?" asked Sebastian.

"Can't tell you that kid," said the voice. The voice clearly was a man. But young or old Sebastian couldn't tell.

"Why should I stay down?" asked Sebastian.

"Because it will save your life," said the man. He sounded exasperated.

"I'll die no matter what out here," said Sebastian. The man chuckled and suddenly Sebastian realized that the voice was young.

"If you stay down you'll live; I've been out here before. I know how to survive. If you want to live you need to do as I say," said the young man. The weight that had been on Sebastian's back lightened and he could get up. He turned on his back and saw a young man staring down at him. Then Sebastian realized that it was the enemy. He scrambled back and grabbed the knife at his belt. Yanking it out he held it in front of him.

"I see you now know who I am," said the young man. He seemed disappointed.

"Though I want you to know that I won't hurt you," said the young man. Holding out his hand he said, "Names Matt, what's your name kid?" asked Mat.

"Sebastian," said he. Sebastian looked warily at Matt.

"Again I won't hurt you. I'll help you survive," said Matt.

"Thanks?" said Sebastian. Matt laughed, "You're welcome kid, follow me I'll show you a safe place to be. And it's also where you can get a lot of the men, they'll never see it coming," said Matt. Sebastian doubted that. Who knows if Matt is telling the truth, is he telling the truth? Or is he lying? And then there was the part where Matt had said, "I won't hurt you," that could be another lie. Was everything in this life a lie? Should he trust Matt? Or was he like all the other men? All liars, thief's, murderers. All of the wicked. All of them greedy. They all want gold. Or fame. While some of them just want to kill their enemies. Do they deserve justice? Or will they go to their deaths? Never to receive their mercy.

Chapter 32

Thirty-second night:

Stella walked through the alley. Three people were following in tow. She had promised that she'd give them a home. Currently, they were heading to her other home. It had been given to her by her father. Her father had known that she was always good. She had been trying to help Gavoth but he was too stubborn.

The house her father had given her was being used for the hungry, cold, and homeless. She wanted to give them hope. But it was hard to give hope in these times. It just wasn't possible. Stella turned a corner ahead she saw the house it was lit as always from the inside. The light from the inside had always made the house look warm and inviting. The young woman and their children gasped in relief.

"Oh thank you, Stella! You're a lifesaver! What would we do without you?" asked one of the women. Her name was, Elodie. She was such a kind girl. She deserved more than she had. She deserved a home to call her own. Elodie ran forward with her children. The other girls followed in tow, smiling. Tears streamed down their faces. Stella smiled in happiness. They deserved it.

"Thank you, Stella! I don't know if I would have survived if you hadn't given us a home and a warm place to sleep," said another girl. She smiled through her tears.

"It's my pleasure. No one should be left on the streets," said Stella. A few of the girls came up and gave Stella a hug. They kept on saying 'thank you'. She smiled she was glad that they were happy.

When they reached the house they heard voices inside.

"Who else is living here?" asked Elodie.

"Other people who needed a home, you even might know them," said Stella. The people in the house had heard Stella walk up to the house. Small faces pressed to the window. The door opened and out came a young woman.

Elodie recognized her immediately. She screamed with happiness. Elodie ran forward and wrapped her arms around the girl. They both laughed with joy.

"How long have you been here Analia?" asked Elodie. The young woman smiled.

"A year. Thanks to Stella she gave fourteen people a home and plenty of food. There are even showers!" said Analia enthusiastically. The other girls gasped in surprise.

"Ok Stella you didn't tell us that there were showers," said Elodie.

"It was meant to be a secret," said Stella.

"Well are you going to come in or are you going to stay outside?" asked Analia at the door. The other young woman stepped inside and gasped as they saw the giant chandelier. have

"I'm glad you like it," said Stella.

"Food is in the kitchen. It's hot soup. Hope you enjoy it," said Stella as she pointed towards the kitchen. The girls headed to the kitchen and saw a giant pot of boiling soup.

"Should we eat right now or get cleaned up?" asked Elodie.

"That's a good idea. Get cleaned up and then we can eat," said Stella. Elodie nodded.

"The bathrooms are that way," said Analia. She pointed towards the stairs.

"Between the stairs," she said again.

Stella noticed that Elodie had stayed behind.

"What's wrong?" asked Stella.

"Does Gavoth know that you being good behind his back? We don't want you to get hurt like last time," said Elodie.

"He doesn't know but I think next week I should tell him. I think it's for his own good," whispered Stella. Elodie nodded and then went into her room. she would tell Gavoth next week that she had no interest in being bad. she just hoped that he'd understand.


Chapter 33

Thirty-third night:

Gavoth was pretty sure that Stella was hiding something from him. But he couldn't figure what the thing she was hiding from him was. Stella had been quiet all evening. Finally giving in Gavoth decided to give her the cold shoulder to see if that would work. It didn't help at all. Gavoth stared at Stella in aggravation why didn't she speak already?

"Okay, seriously why aren't you speaking to me, Stella? Is it something I've done?" growled Gavoth as he slammed his fist onto the table. Stella only watched him with one of her eyebrows raised. That aggravated Gavoth even more. He sat there breathing hard and watching his sister. Still, she wouldn't speak to him.

"My dear sister, what have I done to wrong you? Is it I?" whispered Gavoth. Stella took a deep breath.

"It's not you my dear, I've only been thinking of my day," said Stella.

"It's been a crazy day my dear," said Stella. Right, if that's the problem.

"I know you well. Your hiding something from me," said Gavoth.
"Oh really? I am hiding something from you. But you can't have it. You have the nasty habit of spoiling the fun," she said this with a smirk.
"Oh, that's not fair! I never spoil things," muttered Gavoth. Then he realized that she was right.
"You realize that I'm right," said Stella matter-of-factly.
"Yes I do, but still think it's a bad idea that you won't tell me," said Gavoth.
"You never said it was a bad idea. It never was. I'm doing because I feel it's right," said Stella.
"Fine," said Gavoth as he slumped into his seat defeated.
"You win," he said again. Stella smiled.
"I always win my dear. And you know that for a fact," she said.
"You're probably right," said Gavoth.
"I'm always right. I always win. Always get what I want. Because if I don't get what I want there's going to be trouble," said Stella.
"Of course the motherly part of you kicks in. That's when I need to be careful," muttered Gavoth.
"For the first time, your correct Gavoth. Good job," said Stella. She grinned.
"Stop toying with me," whispered Gavoth. Though the side of his mouth started to rise slowly.
"You know that I love to toy around with you. Mess with your mind," said Stella. This time Gavoth looked up and smirked.
"That has always been your favorite part of being my sister," said Gavoth. He chuckled quietly.
"Yes, It has. It's because I love you," whispered Stella. She put a hand on Gavoth's shoulder and then left the room. but before she left she turned to him and said the most unexpected thing ever.
"I don't want to be bad Gavoth. I should have told you this before but I've been helping some people who don't have homes or food. they're staying at fathers mansion that he gave to me. thought that you should know this," said Stella. then she turned on her heels and walked out of the room. Gavoth stared at the door in shock. She didn't want to be bad? Why was that?
"Yes, you have always loved me. Put yourself before me. Protected me when I did stupid," whispered Gavoth.


Chapter 34
Thirty-fourth night:
Mathew and Aoife walked through the deep, dark forest. It was so cluttered. No sun streamed down through the branches. It was pitch black. It seemed like the forest was going on forever.

This is the enchanted Forest of Eandorel. It grows bigger by the second. Always moving. Always shifting. It's very easy to get lost.

Mathew looked over his shoulder in concern. It felt like he was being followed. But in the darkness even though it was morning he couldn't tell if he was right or wrong. He heard a stick crack behind him. Mathew and Aoife whirled around, no one was there except a small rabbit.
"this forest is seriously giving me the creeps," muttered Aoife. Mathew nodded in agreement, then realized Aoife couldn't see him in this darkness.
"I agree. This forest is very creepy," said Mathew. Over the past few months, Aoife and Mathew had gotten to be best friends. They learned how to rely on each other. To rely on each other's instincts. Sometimes it went well and sometimes it didn't. Sometimes they got into danger.
"Do you know where we are Mathew?" asked Aoife. He had no idea where they were.
"Nope. No clue," said Mathew.
"Do you know where we are?" asked Mathew.
"I have a small hint of where we are. I think we are in the forest of Eandorel. But that can't be possible. According to the weird glowing map, that witch had given to us. It says we are fifteen miles west from the forest," said Aoife. Her voice etched with concern.
"I know where you are," said a voice from behind them. Mathew and Aoife jumped in shock. When had someone come behind them? They turned around but no one was there.
"Where are you?" yelled Aoife.
"I'm right here," said the voice behind them. They whirled around but still, no one was there.
"We can't see you," said Mathew. As always he stated the obvious.

"And how do we know you're to be trusted?" asked Aoife. The voice chuckled. Now right by their sides.

"That is a great question Aoife. And Mathew you're as careless as you were when I first met you. It's good to see you, my dear boy," said the voice.

"How do you know my name. I never told you it," said Aoife. She took a step back, but an invisible wall of air kept her from going any further.

"Mathew do you know what the voice is talking about? Do you know who it is?" asked Aoife. Her voice etched with fear.

"At first I was confused. But now I'm starting to remember who this voice is. It's a man. Very powerful. His name is Balthazar. The sorcerer. The conjurer of demons. He's not to be trusted. He's evil. And... now that I'm starting to remember he was the one who killed my parents," said Mathew. If there was enough light you could tell he was sneering.

The voice of Balthazar was etched in fury. Even though they couldn't see Balthazar Mathew and Aoife could tell that he was pissed off.

"How dare you accuse me of killing your brother! Um... I mean your parents; I never did such a thing! Your parents were my best friends!" said Balthazar. He now appeared in a blinding flash of light. Mathew and Aoife squinted against the harsh light. Once their eyes adjusted they saw Balthazar to who he really was. He wasn't a man. He was an enormous snake.

"See there's our evidence. You hesitated. We know you're lying to us. And no wonder why you know our names you've been following us for the past five miles. But what we want to know is why did you kill Mathew's parents?" asked Aoife. The snake slithered back. Its face etched in panic.

"Uh... from... it's true I killed his parents. They were hunting down my parents. Oh and I'm not really a snake. I thought it would scare you. But I see that didn't work," said Balthazar. He then shrunk down into a small man. A man of tan skin and a sad face.

"Oh dear! Why do you look so sad?" asked Aoife.

"Do you want me to tell you why I killed his parents?" he said this by pointing to Mathew.

"Probably a good idea," said Aoife. She put her hands on her hips.

"Well first of all your parents were hunting me down. Because I tried to take your sister when she was a baby. That made your parents very angry," he paused to let that sink in.

"I have a sister? Where is she?" asked Mathew.

"I'll tell you that later. Now back to the story," Balthazar sat down. He looked up at Mathew and Aoife.

"You might want to sit down. It's going to be a long story," said the old man. They sat.

"Good. So your parents weren't regular humans. They were magicians. But five years ago they died when they were fighting me. They miss-pronounced the spell they were chanting and they burst into flame. Reduced to ashes. But way before you were born we were ancient enemies. We fought great battles. But now that they're gone I miss them. I realize they were my best friends. Even though at times we loathed each other. And at times we didn't get along. I don't know why I followed you. It might be because I miss your parents. Maybe I want a friend," said Balthazar.

"You should have just told us that. We'd be happy to have someone with us," said Aoife.

"Do you know the forest?" asked Mathew.

"Yes, I do know this forest. But beware it's very dangerous. Though I bet you already know that," said Balthazar.

"Yes, we did know that. It's pretty ironic that you said that. We have already dealt with a witch. Her name was Oleander," said Aoife. Balthazar raised his eyebrows in horror.

"You met the witch Oleander? I'm surprised you even survived that encounter. She's very evil. And very cunning. Though at first, you think she's good and she won't hurt you," his voice became bitter. Although it had a hint of sadness.

"And then she hunts you down and burns you to death. It's happened to me. I barely escaped with my life. Though I have the scar for trusting her," he then pulled up his sleeve and showed them a dark red scar, it ran from his thumb to his elbow.

"What happened?" asked Mathew as he leaned forward to get a better look.

"As I said she hunted me down. She hurled fire at me. I rolled away. But the flame got my arm and this side of my body," he motioned to his right side of his body.

"She must have burned you pretty good," said Aoife. Balthazar nodded.

"Did you trust her for a while?" asked Mathew.

"Oh yes. For quite a while she was my best friend. And then I had to leave for a journey. I'm pretty sure she didn't like that. So after a while of being gone, I got a feeling of being followed. And then one night she came to me. I thought she was going to help me find my goal. But I was wrong. She came at me with fury in her eyes. Hurling fire every which direction. She burned me. I haven't seen her since. And don't plan to see her if I can," said Balthazar. Mathew and Aoife nodded.

"We thought she had something weird about her. She kept on referring to a dear friend. She sounded quickly. And also sad when she talked about the 'dear friend'" said Mathew.

"Did she have any other weird quirks?" asked Balthazar.

"Yes. She kept grabbing a small stone. And rubbing it. Is that good or bad?" said Aoife. Balthazar paled.

"She didn't have the stone when I last saw her. when is new," whispered Balthazar. He looked terrified.

"What did the stone look like?" he asked.

"Dark green. With swirls around the stone. And small black and blue spots covering the stone," said Mathew. Balthazar paled even further. If that was possible.

"That is not good. She has possession of the Enderlin Stone," said Balthazar. He had his head in his hands.

"What is the Enderlin Stone?" asked Mathew and Aoife simultaneously.

"It is a stone of great power. It has the power to potentially blow up the world. And maybe the universe. She can't possess the Stone. Even though I have no interest in going to her. I need to get the stone away from her. Do you plan to go to her soon?" asked Balthazar.

"Yes in five days," said Aoife.

"That will work. If it was any longer I'd have to let you travel the forest by yourselves," said Balthazar. He looks less terrified.

"Well we should get some sleep we have a long day tomorrow," said Balthazar. He smiled tiredly at Aoife and Mathew and then laid down and didn't speak for the rest of the night.

Chapter 35

Thirty-fifth night:

Balthazar had pretended to go to sleep but he couldn't. His mind was too worried. His thoughts were flying at a hundred miles an hour. Why had Oleander taken the Enderlin stone? She had mentioned it to him before he had left but then she didn't seem to be that fascinated in the stone. Why did she have it now? It was too dangerous. Maybe he did care for her after all. Balthazar smiled sadly as he lay on the ground he heard the girl and boy talking quietly. He heard the girl whisper, "I'm worried about him Mathew. Did you see what his expression was when we mentioned the Enderlin Stone? I think he truly cares about the witch. He didn't mention how long he was with her, but I think he was with Oleander for a very long time. He loves her Mathew! Don't you realize that?" whispered the girl. The boy, Mathew said, "I think you're right but we shouldn't go into his business. It's not ours to deal with. But you're right I think Balthazar loves Oleander. She might have been good when he was with her but not now she's an evil witch that kills you with fireballs. Don't you think that's a little risky Aoife?" asked Mathew in a hushed tone. She sighed.

"You're probably right," she sighed again, "We should get some rest," said Aoife. They were right they should get some thought. But they should stay in the dark and not know that he'd listened to their conversation. Balthazar waited for the two kids to lay down then he silently got up and walked into the forest. He would hunt down Oleander if he had too. But the two kids would not go with him.

"Balthazar where are you going?" whispered Aoife kindly.

"You don't need to know. No, go to sleep. You'll see me in the morning," whispered Balthazar as he put his sandals on. Aoife obeyed. She lay back down but she kept her eyes open and watched him.

"I said to go to sleep, my dear. You'll see me in the morning," whispered Balthazar.

"I will but I have a few questions for you. You heard our conversation didn't you?" asked Aoife. Balthazar sighed and then nodded.

"Yes. You should keep that information secret," said Balthazar.

"Ok next question. Who are you really? Are you a wizard or are you a servant of Oleander?" whispered Aoife. She had I right to think so but she didn't need the information. He started to walk away but Aoife's commanding voice stopped him dead in his tracks.

"You not going anywhere until you answer my questions," said Aoife she sat up and stared at Balthazar. He felt an invisible rope tighten around his chest. He smiled.

"You have magic, that's good. You'll help me in my mission. You will help me kill someone of great importance," whispered Balthazar. Aoife shook her head.

"I'm sorry I can't help you. I can tell you're not a good person. You want to destroy someone. Make others miserable. I can't help you kill people and then make other people's lives miserable. Now go Balthazar. Go and do your evil deeds. We don't need your help," said Aoife. Balthazar's face twitched in anger.

"How dare you call me evil. I'm doing good. I want to help the world. This world is nothing compared to my world. I will make it mine. And how could you do this I just helped you," Balthazar whispered fiercely.

"You're right you'll make it yours. But also cold and cruel. Devoid of kindness," said Aoife. She was now standing with her hands on her hips. Not surprising since that was her usual stance.

"You didn't help us I used our trust the wrong way. We can't help anymore," whispered Aoife.

"And is your name really Balthazar? Or is it something else. Something also devoid of goodness?" asked Aoife. Balthazar shook in anger. Steam poured off him in waves. So thick that it filled the camp in less than five seconds. Balthazar started to change. Not to the serpent he was before but into a wisp of smoke. A demon. Aoife realized that and ducked just in time as the demon flew at her in a rage. It flew over her head and crashed into a tree. As it crashed into the tree it changed back into the old man Balthazar.

"Fool! You will regret saying all you said. Now die or serve me!" hissed the demon. It flew at Aoife again and she dodged to the right. The demon came at her again. She dodged and ducked. Trying to tie the demon. The demon's movements became slow and sluggish as it continued to catch Aoife. Mathew was still on the ground sleeping unaware of what was happening around him. The demon flew towards Aoife when she was distracted. He caught her in the chest. Aoife flew back and hit a tree. She groaned and fell to the ground unconscious. The demon laughed quietly and then materialized into its human form. But it wasn't Balthazar. Instead, it was like a mix of a snake, bear, lion, and a human. Balthazar grinned down at the still figure of Aoife and reached down and extended a claw. The demon touched the claw to Aoife's shoulder she shuddered in her sleep and a faint light rose out of her shoulder. She gasped quietly and the demon laughed again.

"You will regret doing what you did to my sister. You won't live through next week. I'd be very surprised if you did survive. Enjoy your sleep," whispered the demon in a raspy voice. It then straightened up and walked into the shadows. A figure watched from the shadow's as the demon disappeared. Once the demon was gone the figure emerged from the shadows. The figure in the shadowed was a young man. Black hair as dark as midnight. Eyes as green as the sea. He walked to Aoife. And knelt down. Putting his arms under her body he carefully picked her up then standing up he walked into the gloom taking the unconscious Aoife with him.


Part 36
Thirty-sixth night:

Aoife woke up in a warm bed. Her chest felt tight. Her mind felt like cotton. She tried to sit up but a hand came and pressed down.

"Not yet my dear. You're not healed yet. Rest," whispered a voice from her right. Aoife tried to see who it was but she couldn't move her head. She was so tired. Aoife drifted into the darkness that awaited her. She closed her eyes…


Aoife opened her eyes. She looked around. A young man was slumped in a chair fast asleep. He sighed in his sleep. Then he jerked awake. She flinched in surprise as she saw the color of his eyes. Dark green. Green so deep. His eyes reminded her of the sea. He smiled at her and leaned forward.

"Are you hungry?" he asked. She nodded not sure yet what to say to the young man. He stood up and stretched and then walked out of the room. The room was small the bed warm. She hadn't realized how hungry she was. How long had she been asleep? Where was Mathew? The young man came back into the room with a steaming bowl. She smelled the air. The food he'd brought her smelled so good.

"How long have I been asleep?" asked Aoife. The young man smiled. Instead of answering he handed her the bowl. It turned out that it was soup. Aoife looked closer at the young man and saw that he had pointed ears. An elf! He smiled at her again.

"You should eat. You've been asleep for two weeks. You've woken up a few times to eat. But you haven't come to full wakefulness," said the young man. Two weeks! Why was she here?

"Where am I?" asked Aoife.

"You're at my house. We're in the middle of the forest. I'm surprised you survived the encounter with that demon," said the young man.

"Demon?" whispered Aoife and then the memories rushed in. Aoife gasped as she recalled of what happened.

"Yes, demon. The demon you encountered was named Calthazar. Though he calls himself Balthazar. He's not to be trusted," said the young man. Changing the subject so she didn't have to hear of what happened she asked, "What's your name?"

"Celeborne," said the young man. Celeborne sat back into his chair.

"Can you tell me what happened with my friend? His name is Mathew," said Aoife.

"One of the other elves I was with took him to her house he should be awake by now… would you like to see him?" asked Celeborne. Aoife nodded.

"I'll go get my friend so she can help bring your friend here," said Celeborne. He got up and walked out.

Part 37

Thirty-seventh night:

Aoife was left alone for a while. While Celeborne was gone she tried to get out of the bed. But when she tried to get out of the bed her head rushed with dizziness. She pulled off the covers and grasped her legs were covered in bandages. What happened between her and the demon? Should she ask the elf? The elf entered with another elf. Except the other elf was a young woman. Her hair was like starlight. She had a radiant smile. The room warmed up as she entered the room. Celeborne notices that she had the covers off. He frowned and nudged the elf woman. She nodded.

"My names Arwen. I'm Celeborn's friend. Your friend will be coming in shortly," said Arwen. Her voice was like the rushing waters of a river. Smooth… and feral at the same time. But Arwen talked quietly. Barely a whisper.

Mathew rolled in on a rolling chair. Never seen a chair like that before. Must be an elf invention.

"What kind of chair is that?" asked Aoife. Celeborne smile in amusement.

"It's called a wheelchair. We use it for people who can't walk. Aoife you can't walk," it then occurred to Aoife that Celeborne had known her name all along.

"The demon did a very dangerous spell when you, Aoife, got knocked out. And when your friend was asleep," he looks at Mathew and then back at Aoife, "The

demon Calthazar knocked you out. He put that spell on you. The elves are trying to figure out how to take it off you. But currently it's very challenging," said Celeborne. He seemed sad that it had happened.

"So… what I'm getting from this is that you saved us. Am I right?" asked Mathew as he wheeled in on the 'wheelchair'. Celeborne nods.

"You're right. I was watching from the shadows and then when the demon left I came and got you two. You were lucky that Calthazar didn't do anything worse to you. It would have been harder to pull you from the darkness," said Celeborne.

"Is that a literate term?" asked Mathew. Celeborne smiled but Arwen stayed emotionless.

"Yes, it's literate. We did really pull you from the darkness. When a demon puts a strong spell on a human the human goes into a state of darkness. If they stay in the state of darkness they will die. For their spirits aren't strong enough. But when we tried to pull both of you back your spirit seemed to want to stay there. Do any of you have magic?" asked Celeborne. It seemed like he was the talker between him and Arwen. Aoife and Mathew exchange a glance. Mathew nods.

"Tell them they have a right to know," said Mathew. Celeborne raises an eyebrow.

"We both have magic… but we don't know how to use it… I would guess that's very dangerous," said Aoife. Arwen nodes.

"It's a good thing you told us. Do you know what kind of magic you do when it appears?" asked Arwen. They both shake their heads.

"Ok, that's going to make it a little harder. Let's try another question. Have you used any magic in the past month?" asked Arwen.

"And don't be afraid to answer. We're trying to keep you safe. While there's much evil in the world the elves have always tried to keep the evil at bay," said Celeborne. He smiled encouragingly at them.

"We've used some in the past month. Though it's mostly Aoife. She seems to have the strongest magic. She used it to defend us from these evil red fairies in the forest. She basically drowned them to death. She… leached water out of the air and then poured it on the fairies. They drowned. Does that help?" asked Mathew. The elves didn't answer instead both of the elves had straightened in surprise. Their faces etched in fear and wonder.

"Veelnorks. Water Mages. What is your power Mathew?" asked Arwen. She seemed to be the magic expert.

"I seem to be able to wield fire and storms. For example, I got pretty mad at a wizard three months ago and blew him into the air, with a pillar of air. Then blew him westwards with a stream of fire," said Mathew. Again the elves gawked in fear and wonder.

"Treelnorks. As you said you can control the weather and fire. And one more thing… The. Second element " said Arwen. She stared at them in surprise.

"We haven't had young people with these powers for three millennia. This is very worrisome. Plans have changed we need to take you to the king and queen of the elves. She then will tell us how to train you. Hope this doesn't interfere with your plans. But this is of the highest importance," said Arwen.

Part 38
Thirty-eighth night:

Natasha stared into the inky darkness as William stood in front of her.
"What's wrong?" she whispered.
"Someone's coming, I hear it in the wind. Get behind that pillar of rock," said William quietly.
He motioned to the giant rock pillar. They both ducked behind the pillar just in time two boys
with ragged clothes. One boy had a metal arm, blood was dripping off the polished metal
like water. Coating the stone beneath him dark red. The second boy was bleeding out of one
ear. He looked like he was about to faint from the pain.
"Who are they?" I mouthed. William shakes his head urgently.
"Don't speak," he barely breathed the words.
"These boys are the servants of the Dark Ones. If they hear you they will come and
investigate. If they see you, they kill you. Because the last things the Dark Ones want is to
find out that someone from your world is of theirs," whispered William. He peaked around
the corner and then ducked back behind the pillar of stone.
"Don't move," mouthed William. I nod slowly. A few painfully quiet moments pass and then
he does the 'thumb up' sign.

Part 39
Thirty-ninth night:

for a while, William and I head into the darkness. and then all of a sudden was in a huge
underground tunnel.
"Where does this lead?" I ask.
"It leads to the castle. We keep it hidden because the Dark Ones hunt my boys and me
down," he whispers. I nod. It must be sad to stay in hiding when these Dark Ones are
hunting them down. it must be scary.
"When will we arrive at the castle?" I ask.
"We're already here. Welcome to my home. I like to call it Chocklee it's called this because it
literally chokes the Dark Ones. Or chokes their life away," says William. when he says this
he spreads his arms and quietly says a word. and I suddenly see a huge castle. Lights
glimmer through the darkness. it is so pretty.

Part 40
Fortieth night:
I can't get the image of the boys pounding my small body into the ground. My head throbs
with pain as the boys kick me over and over again. It's the third time they have attacked me
this week. I really don't know what to do. I don't have any money to move away because the
first group of boys stole all I had. I cringe at the sound of the boys laughing. They are so
cruel I wouldn't be surprised if they didn't know the meaning of kindness. I can't get a breath
in my lungs. It hurts so much so I stay silent. The boys don't like that so they kick me harder
than before. That gets me to groan. The boy above me smiles crudely, showing all his teeth.
They are black like tar. I shudder in horror, what have we been through? The boys switch
person. They switch to let each boy get in fifteen minutes of kicking in. I hurt so much. When
I am alone I have time to look at my body. It's covered in black and blue bruises, sometimes
yellow. The skin is torn and my ribs ache. Though it's not surprising that I have broken ribs.
I don't understand why I'm still alive. It's cruel at how long I have lived. I just want to die, but
some unknown force doesn't let me. Apparently, someone wants's me alive. Sometimes I
have woken up and seen someone kneeling by my side and taking care of me. I'll probably
never find out why I'm being saved. Once I even asked, "Why are you taking care of me I'll
just keep getting hurt," but the person just shakes her head and whispers, "Rest I'll protect
you," and then I would fade into the shadows of dreamland. It's scary at what I dream.
Dreams of terror, I hear people scream. children crying, sadness, war, so much war. I don't
know why I'm dreaming the dreams… they might be visions to help me, but I don't see how.

Five weeks later the beating stops and I'm in a small house. I wake up to the smell of herbs, like cinnamon, mint, spearmint, other smells I can't identify. Ash is layered against the ground making it look like fur, but I know it's not Smoke is swirling around my head like mist. I wonder where am. I slowly look around the room a young girl is sitting in a chair sleeping. Seriously where am I? Then I realize I don't feel any pain. Now that's weird. I sniff the girl opens her eyes and looks at me.

"Good you're awake," she whispers.

"Do you know who those boys were?" she asks.

I shake my head. That was a good question. who were they?

"Those boys aren't even close to human. I know this sounds weird but you need to run. you're not safe here," she whispers.

"What are you talking about? And who are you?" I ask. My voice is hoarse from not using it. The young girl grimaces.

"This will sound very weird but I'm from Neverland. I'm the elven queen of Neverland. And those boys are not boys they are called the Dark Ones. They are looking for other children to kill them or make them their slaves. The worst thing that could happen to you is to become their slave. you would never have your freedom. You would be serving them for all eternity. They may look like boys but they're much worse," said the girl.

"Oh and my name is Eleanor," said she. I look at her as if her brains were fungi.

"You. Are. Crazy. Did you drink beer before you saved me?" asked Michael. Eleanor smiles.

"Close enough, in your world. would you like to see my world?" she asks. she has a knowing smile.

Uh oh. Is that good? She leans forward and grabs my arm. and suddenly the world goes black. I have the sensation of falling and then suddenly I'm on a beach. The water is the bluest of blues. Falling memories I vomit. Where am I? Eleanor smiles. I must have voiced my question.

"You are in Neverland Michael," she says.


## Part 41

Forty-first night:

Eleanor is standing over me with a peculiar expression of concern.

"You'll get better. It's just the effect of traveling from world to world. Michael welcome to Neverland," she said waving her hand towards the enormous forest around us.

"You got to be joking me. Are we in Neverland? I thought this place was..."

"Not real?" asked Eleanor. I nodded.

"Well let me tell you right now it's very much real and also very dangerous. You'll stay with me if you don't want to be killed by giant fire-breathing lizards," said Eleanor.

"Yup you are definitely crazy. Why am I here?" I asked.

"I told you are in danger. The Dark Ones are hunting down children to make them do their will," she said.

"Eleanor doesn't even think of saying their names out loud!" said a man's voice. I turned around and saw a giant of a man walking towards us.

"Uh, who is that?" I whispered.

"My father," Eleanor said. She said it with no feeling. Did she hate her father?


## Part 42

Forty-first night:

I was soon introduced to the giant of a man known as "Father." All I got from him was a glance full of loathing. Why was that? I didn't do anything to him. Eleanor's reputation with her father was stiff at best. When we were walking towards the city known as "Lightlee" Eleanor and "Father" spoke only a few words and the words were clipped. What happened between them to make Father and Daughter so hostile towards each other?

There was also the folk of Neverland. They were so queer, the only welcome I got was a stiff nod, and then their faces changed completely, changing from mild tolerance to pure loathing and fear. Why was that? What did the people of my world do to receive such venom? The flowers of Neverland seemed more hostile than the villagers of Lightlee. Even a mere glance sent me shivering, sending icy fingers of dread down my spine. I could feel the raw, unchecked power pouring off them in waves. it was scaring me, I knew without asking that these people were not to be toiled with. I wanted to go home, but where would I go? All the orphans hated me. Last I could remember was that I nearly got killed by some boys. Wait, Eleanor said this boy isn't human. What did she call them? Dark Ones? Yes, that's what they were called. Michael could now remember clearly. The first time Eleanor said the name he'd felt a shiver of icy waves run down his spine. Apparently, this was a name of power.

there still was the matter of having nowhere to go. should he hide in the mountains? no that was silly. he couldn't do that again. so I guess there was no choice but to stay in Neverland and try to win the Peoples favor. Was he truly brave to do that? Was it dangerous? Wait of course it was. he couldn't deny that it was going to be dangerous. He was in a land that he had no knowledge of. win the people's favor. Great idea Michael! So that's what I did for the next ten years I started to gradually gain their love for me. At the end, I was sure they'd love me. I even fought a few wars against the many evils of Neverland. it was scary sure but it was worth it. In the end, I was named Pan of Neverland, the protector of the people. The people appointed me to guard. I chose to protect the queen. I had later found out that the queen was Eleanor. that gave me a burst of energy in protecting her. so for many years, I protected her. five years later Eleanor gave me a truly kind gift. she gave me the gift of immortality. Over the years I had learned to love the queen and she loved me. it had been ten years of greatness. my eleventh year was paradise and then everything shattered. my perfect world is gone forever. Becoming a world of terror and pain. The Dark Ones caught me one-night sneaking into their layer. once they caught me they brainwashed me. I started seeing things that couldn't possibly be real. While inside their reign of terror I was miserable. I yearned to go back to the people I loved and a queen who loved me. and who I loved with all my heart. did she and my people understand that being with the dark ones tore at my heart? making me cry in anguish? My perfect world was gone. Shattered into a million pieces. Over the next few years, I started to despair. Would anyone come and get me from this world of darkness? I fought my hardest even though I knew it was pointless. I knew that it would end in my failure. The Dark ones would always stand at my prison door and laugh. it was horrible. The Dark Ones had me against my will. sooner or later they'd get me to obey me. then it happened my world shattered even more if that was possible. were the devils laughing at me? the dark ones had come to me with a pale yellow dress driving with fresh blood. whose blood was it? Did I know the person who had died? Then the dark Ones told me it was Eleanor's blood she had died while trying to come save me. Why Eleanor? Why did you have to try to save me? This turned my stomach. I tried to block the pain but it came in nauseating waves. My dear Eleanor. Dead too soon. The devils must be truly cruel to do this to me. I couldn't go any further. I was lost without Eleanor. And that was how I turned bad. to go bad is to lose all you cherish. All that you love. That was what happened to me. So for the next fifty years, I served the Dark Ones loyally. Spreading fear. Making whoever killed my precious Eleanor fear me. I even tried to hunt down the one who killed her. But with no avail. And this is how I became Pan. My first name was Peter. But I now don't deserve that name. Peter was a name of love and happiness. So my name changed from love and Happiness to hate and despair. I. Am. Pan.

# Two:

Part 43
Forty-second night:
Circa, beginning of the first millennium of Neverland:
Sebastian opened his eyes to find a young girl staring at him. At first, he was confused and then he was scared. Where am I? He remembered that he was on the battlefield and then that young man, the enemy saved him. Where had the man taken him? He opened his

mouth to say something but he was surprised when the girl stuffed a piece of bread in his mouth. That's when he realized he was starving. He closed his eyes savoring the warm taste of bread. It had honey. He again opened his eyes and the girl was still there. the Sitting against the wall. Sebastian looked around the room. It was a small room with windows. The windows were pouring sunlight into the room making it seem happier than it actually was. He looked at the girl still sitting there. He swallowed the bread and spoke. His voice rusty from not using it.

"Where am I?" the girl shook her head.

"You don't know?" she asked. I shake my head. I put a look of absolute confusion on my face to show how I'm feeling.

"First of all, you fell from the sky. Second of all, you're in Neverland," said the girl matter of factly. I stared at the girl in unbelief. Seriously? Did I really fall out of the sky? I started to laugh and then I noticed the girl's expression. She wasn't kidding. When did I 'fall out of the sky'?

"What's your name? I probably shouldn't refer you to as 'the girl'" I muttered. The girl smiled and for the first time, I noticed she had shark teeth. Creepy.

"My name is Noyatan. I'm from the east region of Neverland. That's where the Mere-People comes from. I thought you should now that since apparently you've never been the Neverland." I nod.

"I seé," she says.

"What's your name? I'm sure you have one," Noyatan said.

"Sebastian, and of course I have a name," I said. Noyatan shakes her head.

"No, no that won't do. You have an earth name. Here on Neverland if you stay you need to adopt a neverlandien name. so names like Pan or Hook. Or Sokat. That's my sister's name. very noble. But you can't have that name since you're a boy. And pan wouldn't do. How about' Hook? Yes, yes I think that'll do greatly Hook," she said Matter of factly.

"But my name is Sebastian NOT Hook. And I don't want to stay here. I need to get back to my family!" I said. She shook her head.

"If you come to Neverland you can't go out. I haven't met anyone who has gone away. Except for the Dark Ones. They can do whatever they wish. They are the prime rulers," Noyatan shudders. What were the Dark Ones?

"The Dark Ones? Oh, their evil they've been enslaving us Neverlandiens for three millennia. Don't mess with them or they'll kill you. Well ok, that's a lie. They'll rip out your guts and feed upon your flesh…. Don't ask. I don't want to say what will befall you if you make the Dark Ones mad. Now shut up Hook! They might be listening," I stared in shock as Noyatan read my mind. How did she do that?

"How did I hear your thoughts?" I nod.

"Well, your thoughts are basically here for me to see. You need to hide your thoughts better. But to do that you'll need training. And to do the training you'll need to find the Queen. She'll help you… maybe," oh that was comforting Noyatan could hear his thoughts. Why did he have to come to this godforsaken place? Oops. Judging by the look Noyatan gave me she did NOT appreciate that. It was NOT a godforsaken Island. Noyatan nods.

"You're right it's not. Neverland is my home. And I love it. It can be dangerous but I still love it. Hook to keep you safe I need to take you to the Queen,", "Do I have your permission?" I nod It's pointless to say anything. Since you can hear my thoughts. Noyatan smirks.

"Well, of course, I can hear your thoughts… I just decided that I can help teach you how to guard your thoughts while we travel to the Queen. I think it's for the best. That's if you want to stay alive. For if you don't know how to protect yourself in Neverland you'll be alive for a few days. Then the Dark Ones will find you," said Noyatan. "And then they'll kill you. And they'll Probably do it the most violent way you can think of," she continued. With an open mouth, I stare at Noyatan in shock but mostly horror. Why?

"Well because the Dark Ones aren't human. Their evil. They do come from this world but they are older than the queen. And the queen is old. Don't mess with her," she said.

"Is she good?" I ask. She smiles.

"Yes, she is… When I was a little girl she saved my life. Well, I was near death and she nursed me back to health. I love her. I don't know what Neverland would do without her. She is so good. So kind. She hasn't a bad bone in her body. She's pure good. Though if you make her mad that's probably a good time to leave Neverland…" Noyatan chuckles.

"The Dark Ones once pissed her off and she banished them to Gavf. That's basically hell in your world it is such a scary place," Has she been there since she says it's so scary?

"And yes I've been there and I have no wish in going back. So continuing with the thought, the Queen banished the Dark Ones to Gavf. Now they don't dare mess with her. In fact, they're terrified of the Queen. If the Queen is even a mile away they can sense her and they are gone in a second. Just poof! So don't mess with her or you'll regret it. I feel sorry for the people who mess with her or make her mad. There's one guy who made her mad and he never came back. Once the Queen cooled off she realized what she did and she tried to look for him in Gavf but there was no sign of him," she shakes her head.

"Sorry, we should probably get you to the Queen. And while we're traveling I'll start teaching you but it's near night. We need to find shelter you do not want to find out what roams around at night in Neverland. Things like... shatale, kakamouran, teledmorn. All are very dangerous that's all you need to know," she said after I gave her a blank look

"So when we find shelter I'll tell you right now DO NOT go outside without me. Or without my permission. Understand?" she asked. I nod. I have no interest in going outside after she mentioned the things that are out there. Once she said the names of the monsters I realized I knew what they were. And knowing that scared me half to death. Noyatan gave me a look of Surprise.

"You know what these monsters are? Are there monsters like these on your earth?" Noyatan asked. I shake my head. Noyatan looks taken aback.

"Then how do you know about these monsters if they're not in your world?" she asked. "Well in school I had a mythology class and these were some of the main monsters. After the class, I realized that some of these ancient people were terrified. With some of the monsters I learned about I've realized that some of the stories they hear are to mainly make them afraid. And they were. They were so scared. They were scared of the dark and what roams in it," I say. She nodes.

"I see your people were scared most of the time," she said. She seemed afraid now to talk to him now that she knew what these monsters were. She nodded. I was right. She took a deep breath.

"We'd better get moving or it'll get too dangerous even for me to protect you," she said. She started walking westward. After a while, we arrived at a huge cave.

"This will do. Get yourself comfortable while I go look for something to eat. And when you sit down don't move an inch or the monsters will hear you. I'm also going to find some wood. I'll be back in three minutes. DON'T MOVE. And DON'T make a sound," she gives me a strained smile and then turns around and walks out of the cave. Hope she finds some food cause I'm hungry...

"Don't worry I'll find food Hook... oh and you'll have to get used to that name. Since people from your world who haven't changed their names will be killed. Sorry to scare you, but it's the rules. I'll be back in a few minutes. Remember don't move," her voice whispers back. "How far can you hear me?"

"You mean how far can I go until it's nearly impossible to talk to you or hear your thoughts? Well, that's a good question. Very far. If you have the right training. Now hush I need to concentrate." Well, I guess I'll now be Hook. Not Sebastian of New Hampshire.

"Ok scratch that was is this 'New Hampshire'" whispered Noyatan.

"It's in the US. Or earth. It's where I come from, It's my home. Also very pretty. Though New Hampshire has very cold winters," I thought. I then realized I really liked talking this way it was easier.

"Yes, it is. I like it too," she whispered.

"I've found food. Wood is near, I'll be back in a one minute. Have you moved?" she whispered.

"Nope,"

"What's this 'nope'?" she asks.

"Just a way of saying no. I know the language doesn't make sense. And that's saying something since I'm from Earth," I think. I hear me a slight chuckle.

"Funny. I would think your language would be easier. Not harder," she whispers. I smile. She has a point.

"I always have a point. I'm a mermaid. I have sharp teeth!" she chuckles.

"No, it means that your right," I think. I try to laugh in my mind but it's harder than it looks. "Why?"

"Why I don't know. Maybe because I know this thought process,"

"Ok 'you've got a point' Hmm. I like it. It's got a nice ring to it, I think I'll use it from now on," whispers Noyatan.

"Your fun to talk too unlike the other people from my world. Their nearly impossible to talk to. They mostly like to use grunts. It's quite annoying,"

"Inhumane?"

"Yes very," I whisper.

"And thank you I'm glad that I'm easy to talk to. You are too," Noyatan whispers.

"I'm back," she whispers. Right as she walks into the cave. She has a bloody lip.

"Are you okay?" Noyatan nods.

"Yes. Just got into a little struggle with one of the creatures out there," Noyatan says.

"You're also limping. That's not good," I say. She looks touched that I said that.

"That's very kind of you, but I think what we should worry about is your own neck instead. You're the one who's not from this world. I need to protect you, not you me," she whispers.

"how about' we take care of each other. Look out for each other?" I say. She smiles.

"if you do that I'll have to teach you how to fight. Cause the creatures out there will do anything to kill a human. They hate them. Well, they hate you. Already word is spreading throughout Neverland, of your fall from the sky. So if you want to protect me I'll need to teach you how to kill," she said. I nod. I already knew how to fight so that'll help a bit. "That's good. What do you know?" asks Noyatan.

"I know how to fight with my hands, my feet. I know how to use a gun, a sword, and a dagger," I say. She looks very impressed.

"What kind of sword?" asks Noyatan.

"Any sword," I reply. Again she looks impressed.

"Good. Martial arts. What kind?" asks Noyatan.

"All," I say.

"Seriously All? Dang! It turns out that you know more than me. I only know the first five. While there is ten," she says

"Hey, that's pretty good. Maybe I can teach you the next five. We can hone our skills together. Teach each other. Want to do this?" I ask. She nods.

"Cool! Let's do this! When do we start?" I ask enthusiastically. I grin. And she grins back.

"We start tomorrow. Tonight it's time to sleep. We'll need rest if we are to teach each other," says Noyatan. I nod.

"Do you have a blanket to keep warm? Because if you don't I have four. We both can have four,"

"Well, I don't have one. But I guess it's good. The blanket I had on my world was terrible. So thin. In the winter I'd always freeze," I say. She nods and reaches into her pack and pulls out four wool blankets. Super thick. She also pulls out the food she went out and found.

"Will these two blankets work for you?" she asks.

"Oh yes. This will work great. What did you get for the food?" I ask.

"Mntellk," she said. I give her a blank look.

"A kind of bird. It's bigger than you," I stare in shock. Noyatan pronounced 'Mntellk' as Mint elk.

"As big as me? That's a huge bird," I say.

"Bigger than you Hook. Much bigger," said Noyatan. She pulls the meat out, and she was right it was huge! It was so big she had to ask me for help.

"How did you kill this thing?" asks Sebastian.

"with magic. It's the only way to do it," says Noyatan.

"Magic? There's magic here?" I ask.

"Yes. Actually, there is so much magic in this world that some of it leak into your world. And you see it as natural disasters. Like fires, whirlwinds, earthquakes. And much, much more," says Noyatan. Noyatan waves her hand and a white wisp of curls around her fingers.

"Can people from my world learn how to do magic?" I ask.

"Well, you've got to have a parent from Neverland that has magic themselves to have it pass to you as a child. And you'd know if you had magic. You'd be accidentally caching things on fire, exploding things. Leaving things in your wake in disaster, so it would probably be unlikely that you have magic. And also people who have magic are brought to Neverland and trained,", "And If you did get magic randomly I would be very surprised. For it never happens. It only happened once and that person killed herself. Since she was so dangerous," explained Noyatan.

"Actually just to be sure you don't have magic wave your hand three times. If you do have magic the air would shimmer and most likely I'd be pushed back and I'd fly into the wall," said Noyatan. Doing as she asked I waved my hand through the air three times. Nothing happened. Then all of a sudden Noyatan flew into the wall and there was a defining crack of thunder and a blinding flash of light. I yelp and jump up to help her but Noyatan holds up her hand and says, "don't move an inch Hook. We need to talk," I thought she'd have a glare on her face but instead she has a huge smile. That confuses me. What in the world happened? Do I have magic?

"Yup! You do and you're very, very, very powerful! That is awesome Hook not bad! It'll make it easier to protect us. In turn to teaching you how to fight I get to teach you how to fight with magic. And since you're so powerful this is even better! I'm so excited!!" says Noyatan excitedly. She grins. Her shark teeth gleaming in the firelight.

"This is good? But I thought you against the wall! I could have hurt you, and I have no wish to hurt you. Now that we've become friends," I say. She smiles.

"That's good. If you don't want to hurt anyone you won't turn bad. But I have a question who is your mother and father?" asks Noyatan.

"My mother is Sophia. And my father is… I don't remember my father," I say.

"Is that bad?" I ask.

"Nope! It's very good since I know your mother and father. Your mother was the previous queen of Neverland and you father was king. Both of your parents were or are… are they still alive?" asks Noyatan. I nod.

"Awesome. So since their alive, most of their power is flowing to you in a never-ending source. They, in turn, get their magic from the universe. Your parents are probably the most powerful, most awesome people I know! I love your parents! Their actually my best friends!" she is now basically jumping up and down with excitement! I smile. She is so happy.

"Oh yes, I'm very happy. Well drunk with happiness. And this means that you are the rightful heir to the throne of Neverland,", "Any more questions?" asks Noyatan.

"Well, I don't think so. Just a lot of things to take in right now. So let me sum this up. I have magic. My parents are very powerful. In fact, they are the most powerful people known to Neverland, I'm their son. And my power is coming from them through a never-ending source or power. And lastly I'm the heir to the throne of Neverland, did I get everything?" I ask.

"Yup!" she squeaks.

"so we also start magic training tomorrow?" I ask. She nodes.

"Yup! Or the best I can do. I'll do my best," she's now calmed down to a medium instead of a major high of excitement.

"Now we seriously need to get to bed. It's past watch hour!" she smiles at me and then she lays down and closes her eyes.

"You should probably get some rest instead of thinking all night of what I've told you. I know it's a lot to take in but tomorrow you'll be glad that you got some sleep. But if you can't fall asleep I have a spell that'll make it so your mind'll calm down," she whispers.

"I think that's probably a good idea. Will I get a full night's sleep with this spell?" I ask.

"Yes," says Noyatan in a sleepy voice. She waves her hand and immediately I close my eyes and fall into a deep sleep.

Part 44
Forty-third night:

by the fifth day, Noyatan and I had arrived at the castle of the queen. she came strolling down the golden stairs in fair robes of silk. she smiled at Noyatan and saying, "Noyatan how good to see you this day! What brings you here to my kingdom?" Noyatan smiles in return and bows deeply.

"I have come in return of the boy who was foretold of the legend. he is here," she says this while gesturing to me the queen gives me a quick look and then brings her gaze back to Noyatan.

"This is the boy foretold in the legend? The boy who has great power? He who shall overthrow the Dark Ones?" The Queen looks hopeful at this one. Noyatan shrugs.

"I dearly hope so. He does have power but he's never used them before.

And," Noyatan leans forward and whispers, "he doesn't know anything about our world," the Queen raises her brows in surprise.

"How could he not? Did you not say that he was the 'chosen one'?" whispers the Queen

"I did yes, but to be truthful I don't know if he's the right one," said Noyatan with an embarrassed smile.

"I was thinking that if we train him in our ways we might know the truth. Know if he is the one," said Noyatan. I start to walk towards a comfy looking chair to sit in

but Noyatan grabbed my arms and looks briefly at me. In that brief moment, she shakes her head and whispers, "Probably not a good idea to go tromping around trying to find a seat, this place is too dangerous," I tilt my head in confusion. What was that for? Was I not allowed to sit in that chair? then my questions are answered. what I mistook as a chair rose up and walked away. becoming a small girl. she notices me staring in awe and gives me a smirk. I feel a tug at the back of my mind and then I hear a small voice.

"I see your new to this world. Were you going to sit on me?" I then realize the voice I hear is from the small girl. I slowly nod. and give a sheepish grin. She continues to smirk.

"Well, probably not a good idea. My name is Arielle but you may call me Ari since now we've met you now know me. What's your name Human?"

"Sebastian but the woman at my side," I start to say,

"Noyatan yes. I know her very well. She's a dear friend of mine. tell her I can teach you magic. The Queen says she can't teach you, so you must be Hook. Noyatan told me of you on the night she went hunting for food. she said your kind," says the quiet voice. as suddenly as it appeared in my mind the voice left. The girl turned around and continued to walk, before passing out of sight. what an interesting girl. I then turn back to Noyatan she is giving me a strange look.

"Who were you talking to?" she whispers. Since it's apparent that she doesn't want the Queen to hear I whisper,

"I was talking to a girl named Arielle but she said to call her Ari. She said to tell you she's willing to teach me magic since the Queen doesn't want to teach me," she raises her brows in shock.

"Really? Ari said yes. Wow. The last time she and I talked she nearly tried to kill me. tried to shove a flaming tree into my skull. she's known to be very violent," says Noyatan simply.

"Wait, she said you were a dear friend of her's," I whisper. Noyatan looks confused and then a look of absolute terror crosses her face.

"What's wrong?" I quietly ask.

"This is not Ari we're talking about. You just met one of the most dangerous creatures in Neverland. You've just met Doeklamentee, The Demon Slayer. I'm quite surprised that he didn't attempt to truly scoop out your thoughts. cause if he did you'd be long gone. you'd be babbling like a stupid fool. And I'd have to drag you to our next destination. but it's too weird he said that he'd teach you Magic. he does know magic and he's the most powerful creature of all time. but he hates Earth. he has been planning to exterminate the people of your world for centuries. unless he's had a change of heart which I highly doubt . he's so evil. he wouldn't want to change. so why would he want to teach you?" she mumbled.

"I think we should give him, or it, or whatever this guy is; a chance. Let's see if he's actually telling the truth," I say. Noyatan gives me a look like, you have just lost your marbles!

"What are you crazy?! He'll probably kill us!! then eat us for dessert! why would you want to take Magic lessons from a guy who killed his own family in cold blood?" , "Yes, Hook he really did that. He first killed his mother, then his first sister, then his second sister, then he raped his third sister and then drowned that one. Then he choked his brother and father. This guy is purely bad. he's a nut. He even scares the Dark Ones, he's so bad. That's saying a lot! if you can scare the Dark Ones who in themselves are pretty bad, that's how you can tell when you're very evil. So please don't go to him," said Noyatan desperately. I shrugged my shoulders.

"Then who'd teach me magic? No offense but you're putting off the vibe that you don't want to teach me. So I think this evil dude is our best bet," I say. Noyatan looks put out, "Fine you win. We'll go to Doeklamentee, The Demon Slayer. Even though I think it's a horrid idea. Probably the worst idea you'll ever make," she says.

"Alrighty! Let's be off. Which direction to the lair of Doeklamentee?" I say enthusiastically. "That way," says Noyatan glumly as she points west.

"Follow the road, I'll help you along the way if you get lost. Though most likely you will get lost."


Part 45
forty-fifth night:


Noyatan was right we did get lost I had to backtrack our trail three or four times. By the time we actually got to the lair of Doeklamentee it was midnight. Then I found out that the lair is very creepy. Full of 'Goulies and hornpipes'. Or that's what Noyatan said. She had been looking terrified the whole way here. And I kept saying to her, "Relax nothing is going to hurt us," she just gave me the look of impending doom. like you are the one who will die when we get attacked. so now it's midnight and I have no clue how to get into the lair of Doeklamentee. then our heroes came. or one that came in the form of a giant fire-breathing lizard. I ran for my life fearing the worst. nothing happened the dragon just sat there looking at us like we were crazy. then it spoke to us. if our day couldn't get any weirder it just did. by a lot.

"You must be Hook, I'm the one you're searching for. and Hook you can come out of hiding, I'm not going to kill you. Even though you smell very tasty," My heart is running a marathon. why should I trust this thing? He said I can come out of hiding. were is Doeklamentee?

"I am Doeklamentee," the dragon said simply. Staring past the rock he was hiding behind, Hook looked incredulously at the dragon.

"I'm pretty sure that your NOT Doeklamentee. Doeklamentee is a small girl. Or that's what I saw when I met her," said Hook.

"Well I can see that you don't believe me so, I will be forced to show you who I actually am," said the dragon. he then started to change before his eyes. First, he was a dragon and he was a small girl. He was a young man.

"As you can see I am Doeklamentee. I prefer to change my shape. It's more comfortable," said the young man.

"As I am before you I am Doeklamentee. and all the stories you've probably heard about me are wrong. I did not kill my family. someone else killed them. I have no wish to hurt the people from your world. In fact, I had a best friend from Earth. But she died long ago," said Doeklamentee sadly.

"So are you still willing to teach me?" I asked. The young man nodded.

"Yes, I'll teach you. It's the only way for you to stay alive in my world," said Doeklamentee. "Though you will call me Matt. I'm the one who saved you during the war on Earth," said Matt. I stared at Doeklamentee in shock. he was the one who saved me during the war? Did he live here?

Part 46
forty-sixth night:

After finding out that Doeklamentee was actually Matt the young man who saved me in the Barracks I was actually very willing to learn from him. The lessons had been going for five hours. Hook struggled to stay awake as Matt talked about the basics of Magic. the 'lair' of Matt was warm and cozy. and it made it worse that Matt had just given him a warm bowl of soup. Hook also found out that Matt was a very good cook. he made a mean soup. The soup warmed his body and made his mind sleepy. Hook slowly blinked. was Matt growing horns? no that couldn't be he was human...

"Hook wake up!" said a voice. Hook jerked up, looking around.

"What happened?" he asked

"You fell asleep while I was teaching you. Was it my famous soup?" asked Matt. I nodded. I felt horrible. Why had I fallen to sleep while Matt taught me?

"It was very tasty," said Hook absentmindedly.

"Yes, I've been told that. And it's very normal for my famous soup to make you fall asleep," said Matt.

"Ok, that's comforting. I probably fell asleep because I had been traveling.... can we go over what you taught me last night?" I asked. Matt nods.

"Sure, I actually didn't get too far with the teaching. I expected you to fall asleep. So I planned a short lesson. I was done when you fell asleep. So today we'll start over and learn the basics of magic. Then I'll have you demonstrate your skills of magic. Even if you haven't practiced," said Matt. I nod.

"Were is Noyatan? I haven't seen her for a while," I asked.

"She's outside practicing her magic. She's very good," said Matt. "Come see her practice I actually think this will help," said Matt leading Hook outside. indeed Noyatan was good at magic. she threw daggers of fire at stumps of woods reducing them to ash. she had a terrifying look about her.

"Don't distract her when she's in the fighting mode, it could get us killed" whispered Matt when Hook stepped forward. Hook looked back at Matt, then stepping back he continued to listen to Matt.

"Why are you whispering?" asked Hook.

"I'm speaking quietly because it would be hard to concentrate if we spoke loudly. She could hurt us," he whispered again. I again nod in understanding. Then turning on his heals Matt goes back into the house. follow me, we'll start in the back where the sun warms us. I follow him into a sunlit room he was right it was nice and cozy in here. we'll first start with the positions for magic. crossing his legs he plumped into a bean bag.

"Sitting with the back straight will make it easier to stay awake. And will help your power flow smoothly, from Juncktra to Juncktra, that's your energy points in your body," said Matt.

Following the teacher, Hook too sat in the plump chairs. When he came in contact with the chair Hook immediately felt static run through his body. Jumping up he looked at the chair and then to Matt.
"It just shocked me!" said Hook. Matt smiled.
"It didn't shock you. You just felt the flow of your power. If it hurt that means your very powerful," said Matt.
"Oh," said Hook feeling stupid.
"Don't feel stupid. Your not. Many students have felt that shock. Just not as strong as you did. and everyone makes mistakes that don't mean you can too. you can make mistakes. Mistakes are good for you, they help you learn," said Matt kindly.

Part 47
Forty-seventh night:

The next morning Matt said he had something to show me so following him outside we started to walk to town. it took about half an hour to walk to the town. once we got there I stared around in shock. it so beautiful. then Matt pointed to a giant tree with gold and silver tree.
"That is the singing tree in sings some pretty poetry. I think you should ask her to sing to you. It's definitely worth listening to," said Matt as he pointed to the tree from across the square.
"Wait, she? The tree is a she?" I asked in shock. Matt smiled.
"Yup! It's a singing, talking female tree," said Matt
"She's about your age," he added absentmindedly.
"Go on and talk to her. It's actually something I enjoy. She won't bite you," said Matt. I then noticed girls face in the tree. Matt was right she looked to be about his age. Hook slowly walked up to the tree and when he came right in front of her she opened her eyes. Her eyes were a pale gold with flecks of blue and silver throughout the irises.
"You must be new here, my name is Sauna. And I already know your name, you are Hook. You're destined to be a great fighter. you will save many, and gain many lovers. You will see the pain in your life as you seek out the truth of your past life," she whispered.
"Sit by my side and I will tell thee great things, things that have come to past and things that will come to pass," whispered Sauna. I did as I was told and sat in the lush grass by her.
"Do you wish to hear Poetry?" she asked again. Her voice was soft. It sounded like wind in the trees and grass. And waves crashing against the water. It was very soothing to listen to her voice as it swayed from branch to branch. The sun melted down on his face as she started to recite poetry. He recognized some of the poems from his world. and he smiled as he remembered some of his friends from that world coming to him and telling him of the great library full of poetry and other wonderful things.
"Hook." He looked around for the voice but saw nothing. Then a young woman stepped into view.
"who are you?" he asked. she smiled.

"I am the tree. I am the elf that abides there. I am Sauna," said Sauna. Her voice was exactly the same as the tree but her voice was more focused than the tree.

"I have come to warn you. you are in grave danger. The teacher who is slowly drawing near to you seeks to slit your throat. do not trust him. only trust yourself and the merpeople. the Merpeople will help you," she then held out her hand and a small seashell appeared in it.

"This shell will help you stay safe from the man who wishes to kill you, again don't trust him," whispered Sauna.

"Can I trust you?" I ask. Sauna smiles sadly.

"Yes but I'm afraid that if Matt comes to me he will take control of me," she said. then realizing what she said Sauna put a hand over her mouth.

"Ah, fudge! I was not supposed to reveal that to you yet!" She said quietly. She looked as if the world was about to end.

"Wait for Matt? My teacher? Is he going to kill me? I wonder why he hasn't done so yet. He's had so many opportunities. Like when I accidentally fell asleep when he was teaching. When he served dinner to me..." I said then I stopped. Sauna had a look of panic in her eyes.

"Ah, are you okay?" I asked. she shook her head and smiled.

"Yes, just a slip of the tongue. But no need to worry... well okay maybe a little. Oh! Let's just get this over with!" she grumbled. Sauna had a slightly annoyed look about her.

"So let me get this straight, you are like some kind of oracle? right? And you accidentally let a prophecy of me slip through your fingers?" I say. Sauna nods. she has a sheepish smile on her lips.

"Yes. But..."

"No buts. You probably just saved my life!" I said gratefully. I smiled.

"Well, that still puts a damper on things Hook. There's still a probability that you will get killed by Matt," she said. I sighed.

"well is there a way you can help me. Like a way for him not to kill me?" I asked. She glanced at me through her dark bangs.

"I'm a tree Hook, I'm pretty sure that they don't walk out of the ground and make it so that someone doesn't kill someone else. that's impossible... well now as I think about it. it could be possible. I originally was an elf. I could if I had enough strength walk out of the tree and help you. but it is also very, very dangerous to walk out of my home. I only did it once. and that nearly killed me. The chieftain of elves had to heal me back into the tree... Is it worth nearly killing myself to help you?" she pondered. I stared in shock as she talked about what happened when she stepped out of the tree. Was it safe for her to do that? I then have an image flash in my mind. An image of me kneeling by a young woman who had just stepped through a tree. Could this be her? I see myself whispering to her. She nods. She grabs my hand and I pull her up. I see her face. It's definitely the Sauna I see before me. Then the image fades and I know see Sauna. she has a worried look on her face. I touch my face and it's cold.

"I just saw myself with you.... I was helping you." I whisper.

"When was this?" I ask. I don't need to ask if it's real because before she answers another image passes through my mind. of me holding Sauna to my chest. she's crying. sobs raking through her. then the image fades and another comes. an image of me kissing Sauna. she smiles up at me and I am about to see her laugh when the images are gone. I step back in shock where are these images coming from? Then before I can ask Sauna what's happening I see my self. Sauna is before me and I hear her speak,

"Hook you need to go to Earth. It's too dangerous here! Go! Hook I will see you soon. Here's a warning; when you see me you will not know me," tears are streaming down her face as she explains what is to come. Then I nod and turn away fading into darkness. I feel a deep pain in my chest as I tun and leave. All I want to do is turn back and kiss Sauna, but I know I can't. I have a mission on this 'Earth'. I then remember traveling to Earth-living my youth. I then came back here. To Neverland. As fast as the images came they are gone and I see Sauna's panicked face. And with her face a flood of memories. Me fighting for my life as the Dark Ones try to kill my family. Me crying at my mother's side as she slowly bleeds to death. And I'm holding my sister in my arms as she slowly bleeds to death. I feel anger towards the Dark Ones; they killed my family and left me with nothing. Me being crowned as king of Neverland. I see myself riding to war. In front of me, I see a vast army. Full of creatures I before had never seen. But as the images and memories flash through my head I realize I was respected by the people. I was their king. Then I see my downfall. Me killing a young woman named Earasibith. I realize she had been a friend of mine. Why had I killed her? She was such a good person. She didn't deserve to be killed. I then realize she's one of my maids. I watch in horror as my henchmen slice off her head. I'm now shaking in sadness as I realize what I did. Why did I choose such an evil life? I first started as a good man. Then I became a slave of greed. Finally, the images stop and I see Sauna crying before me. I kneel down and lift her chin.

"Oh, my dear Sauna. I've missed you," I whisper. Sauna looks up at me in shock.

"You have your memories back?" she whispered. Her pale face is now full of hope. I nod. She slowly smiles and then slowly stands. then her smile fades. I know where this is going. But to my surprise, she just asks a question.

"What was your first order of being king?" she asks. That's easy I made Sauna a free person, not someone who had to follow the commands of the people. She could choose to tell her poetry or refuse to help the people. When I voice my answer she nods. She grabs my face and kisses me. It's wonderful to be home.

"Now tell me how did you get your memories back so quickly. you should have your memories back in three days time," said Sauna as soon as she let go of my face. Though I noticed that she frequently kept slowly moving her hands up towards my face and then bringing them down.

"Well, I did a small spell to make my memories come back. Now I have all of them," I say. She smiles.

"Now where is that man who betrayed me. Who made me look like a fool?" I ask.

"He's dead. But I have something you need to know. So you know how you were blamed for killing Earasibith? She's sadly very much dead. But it wasn't you who killed her. It was Matt," she said sadly. I stare in shock at Sauna.

"Are you kidding me? Matt killed her? That little traitor! I gave him a lot of power to keep our secret safe!" I growl. She smiles sadly.

"Well, he should be waiting for you, when you wake up. He's actually standing at the foot of my tree with a silver knife," says Sauna.

"Do your worst," I whisper to her. she shakes her head.

"You have to do that. You know as well as I do that it's the rule of my people to not hurt your kind. for if I did hurt Matt your people would burn my home," she says. I nod.

"Right I need to remember that. I guess it's weird having my normal thoughts with me. After not having them for eighteen years," I say. Sauna smiles.

"And who else are we having trouble with?" I ask.

"I'll tell you when you awake. Just press your hand into my side and awake me. I think it's about time for you to do that," she says. I nod.

"It's been too long with the rule of the Dark Ones. We will put them to rest," I say. She nods.

"Now wake," she whispers. The world around me fades and I see Matt slowly raising the knife to strike. I sit up and with a power that feels perfect I say, "Enough Mathanial!" I say as I stand up. My voice is full of power. I am finally home.


Part 48

Forty-eighth night:

Mathanial jumps back with shock as I utter those words.

"Y-your majesty? Hook?" he has a panicked look in his eyes.

"Well of course. Who do you see before you? A clown?" I growl. Mathanial shudders.

"No your majesty. You are not a clown," he says as he looks down at his hands. he then realizes he has the knife still in his hands. With a panicked expression, he throws the knife down. It hits the ground with a dull thunk.

"I heard you betrayed me. you were the one who killed Earasibith. am I not right about this," I ask. again the panicked expression crosses Mathanial's face. He shakes his head and starts stepping back. But I snap my fingers and Mathanial trips. I walk over to him. He's on his back and looking terrified. I kneel on the grass by his side. I sigh.

"What am I going to do with you? You killed one of my friends and made it look as if I did it. Why did you do this?" I ask. He looks away from my gaze but I grab his jaw and forced him to look up at me.

"I know this is not what you want to hear, but I'm saying this for your safety, do you understand?" I ask. He nods.

"Good,"

"I will never hurt you Mathanial. But there are times like this that I need to punish you. As the king of Neverland, I tell you this, you will have to work in the salt mines for three years. And Mathanial this is for your best," I whisper. he stares at me for a few seconds and then he nods.

"I'm sorry. The Dark Ones told me if I did this they'd spare my life. and not kill my family. I couldn't let my wife and my daughter I, I love them too much," says Mathanial. I nod.

"I'm glad you told me this. For that, your years in the mines will only be two years. But still, it'll be very hard, can you withstand the trials of the mine?" I ask. Mathanial nods. I stand up and hold my hand down to him he grabs my hand and I pull him up. Then he does something I did never could have expected, he hugs me. I smile and return the hug.

"Stay good and stay kind Mathanial. Cause I know there is so much good in you," I whisper. He nods.

"What is your plan now that your back?" asks Mathanial.

"I hope you understand this but since you're going to the mines I can't tell you that. I fear the Dark Ones will pester you to tell them what my plans are," I say.

"I understand," he says.

"Now I'll transport you to your home. My best guard will come and pick you up in the morning. He'll be there at ten in the morning. Be ready to leave," I say. I grab Mathanial's hand and in a split second, he's gone. When he disappears I turn to the tree.

"It's finally time to wake up my dear," I whisper. as I say these words the tree shudders. I smile. When the tree stops shuddering I lay my hand on its side and breathe deeply. Then with a commanding voice, I say, "Arise Sauna! Nestunta norvana glaunast ust!" and with a great wind the tree opens up and a young woman walks out of the tree. As she steps out into the light the tree closes behind her and remains as it had been for three millennia. The crowd that had been gathered gasps in awe. A few people clap. The crowd needs no more encouragement they burst forth in wild cheers. I hear a few people calling my name and I smile. I am home with my people. they welcome me home with loud praise. I turn to the people. and smile.

"My people! I am finally home! and with my return, I will help you defeat the Dark Ones! they will regret coming forth from their hell and enslaving us! they will soon slumber!" I yell. The crowd yells with renewed energy. I smile, as I walk through the crowd they continue cheering my name. When I am out of sight from the giant crowd I turn my face toward Sauna. but I then realize it is not Sauna. it is one of the Dark Ones disguised as her. I shake his hand off my arm and glare at him. in return Dourthok the Dark One. The leader of the evil. He smiles up at me. I see his black tongue and yellow teeth. I snarl at him. Dourthok grins.

"Were is sauna?" I growl. the dark One's grin grows even bigger as I ask the question.

"Where is she?!" I yell. I few people look my way and they see that I have cornered the Dark One they scream and run away. Dourthok laughs wickedly.

"Oh, your true love Sauna has been dead for a very long time. If you want to see her body I will take you to it," whispers Dourthok. My world reels. How could she be dead? I just talked to her.

"Oh she's dead alright she was a pretty thing wasn't she?" says Dourthok. Then the world stops. he killed her. The Dark One killed my friend my love. I turn my face towards the Dark One and snarl.

"You killed her!" I whisper harshly. He grins.

"Oh yes it a pleasure in killing her," he says. I growl and grabbing at the power within my body I kill him with a black blade of anger. He screams and falls back onto the ground. I look around and I see a few people huddling in groups. Fear is in their eyes. I hear whispers.

"Who did Hook kill?" I hear. But I pay no heed to the whispers. My love has been killed. My dear Sauna. I take a shuddering breath and take a step forward but I fall on my hands and knees. My world reels and then goes black. There is nothing. I have nothing to live for... I am nothing without her...

Part 49
Forty-ninth night:

I wake up to find my world filled with candlelight. I see a young woman sitting in a chair before me she is watching me with a worried look. When she notices I have my eyes open she sighs in relief.

"Oh good, you're awake! A few people came to my home with you in their arms. Apparently, you killed one of the Dark Ones. but you used too much power. that's why you blacked out. Hook as your friend and healer I order you to not move from this bed until you are fully healed," says the healer. I sigh.

"How long has Sauna been dead Marry?" I ask.

"When did you find out?" asks Marry.

"When I attacked the Dark One. He was the leader. And I'm sure I don't need to repeat his name. he doesn't deserve that much respect. he killed Sauna. He referred to Sauna as 'it'" I whisper. Marry shudders.

"I'm sorry you had to go through that," whispers Marry. I smile sadly.

"I had hoped I would be married to her when I came back from Earth, But I was wrong," I whisper.

"What was the magic you used to kill the Dark One?" asks Marry.

"Blade of anger," I say. Marry looks terrified.

"Are you sure?" she asks. I nod. She shudders. She has a look of doom around her, I wonder briefly if this blade of Anger is a bad thing.

"So what is this Blade of Anger?" I ask. Marry glances at me.

"You don't know what the Blade of Anger is?" she asks. I shake my head.

"Well let's just say it has the power to destroy worlds without number. It's very dangerous and very evil. I'm quite surprised that you did it," she whispers. Now I can see why she was scared this Blade of Anger is truly evil.

"Why did I see Sauna in the dream world and then she wasn't alive when I came out?" I asked.

"I'm not entirely sure Hook. There are a lot of things in this world that are better left unsaid. But my guess is that she left her last memory for you in her world," said Marry.

"When did she die?" I asked. My heart squeezes in pain as I remember her.

"She died three years after you left. She fought bravely. You'd have been proud of her," whispered Marry. A tear rolls down my face as Marry said this. Why did she have to leave me? I needed her. I needed her to strengthen me.

"What happened when I was gone?" I asked. Marry sighs.

"A lot happened while you were gone. Twenty Dark Ones have now been ruling. You just killed one. And from what you said you killed one of the leaders. There are five leaders. The Dark Ones have been running wild through the land and killing anyone they want. we've had about three thousand people killed. Now there are only four thousand in your land. I'm so glad that you have returned home. We need you to get rid of the Dark Ones. it's about time to kill them," says Marry sadly. I nod.

"Your right. It's definitely time to hunt these fools down," I whisper. I try to smile encouragingly at Marry but I fail. I just end up frowning.


Part 50
Fiftieth night:

By the time I'm fully healed and able to walk again it had been three weeks. Three weeks was way too long. By staying in bed for that long I had acquired bed sores. After I had acquired some strength to move I got up in bed and walked into the kitchen.

"Ah you're awake!" said Marry happily.

After I had acquired some strength to move I got out of bed and walked into the kitchen.

"Ah you're awake!" said Marry happily.

"Yes I'm awake, what happened while I was bedridden?" she shakes her head.

"nothing happened my king," said Marry in a choked voice. But I knew she was lying.

"I know there was something that happened. And as your king, it's your duty to tell me. So I can keep the people safe," I say. She mutters something under breath.

"Fine, one of the Dark Ones killed one of our children. she was only two years old. He... he im... impaled her and hung her head on a sp... spicket. It...it was cruel," she muttered. She shakes her head and turns away from me. Before she turns away I notice a tear run down her face. It must have really affected her.

"I promise I'll do everything in my power to stop the Dark Ones," I whisper. She nods.

"Thank you Hook, you are a good king, and always will be," she whispers. I smile. I think she'll be a good counselor for my court.

"Will you be willing to be a counselor of my court?" I ask. Marry turns a shocked face towards mine.

"Are you sure?" she asks. I nod.

"I can't be more sure Marry," I say. She smiles.

"It would be an honor, my king," she says.

"Thank you," I say. She nods and returns to cleaning dishes. I knew I'd have to fight the Dark Ones soon but first, I'd have to recover my strength and gather forces. And when I did they'd never see me coming. The Dark ones will regret taking the kingdom I loved. And taking Sauna. They will pay for all the evil they have spread across Neverland. They will know me. They will know my name. My name is Hook. Captain Hook.

The End.
A Shade of Goodness by Captain Hook


A Tribute to Sauna the Oracle:

I hear the birds singing
 Singing sweetly
The voice flits through a tree
With a happy dance
The morning dawn approaches
The sun streams down on her face, like a river of light
Her auburn hair streams down her face
I hear her singing
Singing sweetly
I smile
I grin
I can't help to have an ecstatic grin!
I smile
I simper
I dance
Through the moonlight, we flit
I sigh
we flit, like birds alight
Through the light, I flit
I sigh
Oh mother how I love you
You make me smile
You make me laugh
I simper
I smile
Oh how I love you
I love the sun!
Sun, sun oh how I love the sun!
She lets her rays stream down my face
If I turn she's on my back always there for me
As I run
 I turn
I turn and smile towards the sky
With a joyous feeling
I skip
I skip
I'm in love
I love
I love
My heart beats in a timed motion
I smile up as her as she brushes my cheek
Her hand is as soft as a feather
I smile
I sigh
I am in love

The sky is blue!
Robin blue
A robin flits through the air
My heart goes with it
My heart leaps with a giddy joy
My heart is with her
My heart is with her
My heart is with her
The rolling plains
The towering mountains
The sky will be blue
If I don't call for you
Oh the stars how they glitter
They glitter with a gleeful light
Calling for me

Calling for me
Always for me
Always for me
She's calling for me
She gives me a gift
A gift of splendor
She hugs me tight
Always close to me
I sigh with wonder
I always will be lucky to have her
Lucky
My love
Oh my love
My love
How you shine
You shine your way through the darkness
Shining your way for me
When I'm blind you show me the way
The sky
The sky
The sky
Oh how blue
She is so blue
The blue of the sea
Or the blue of a robin egg
I see her beauty
It's shining through
Sway with me
Stay with me
I feel your cool air
The spicy scents
Through the air
It's blissful how you make me feel
I feel free when you are near
I can't help but simper at your glorious sight
How warm you make me feel
Your sun is at my back always keeping me warm
Even though the nights are cold
I always see the stars wheeling above
Summer
How you make me shiver!
You are cold
You are brutal
How dreadful you are!
You are near
You would drag on for many nights
Not stopping for a rest
You leave corpses at my door
To signal that we are through
You leave frost at the window
And when I try to get you near you melt at my touch
You are fragile
You are sorrow
You are winter
With your towering red cliffs
Your spacious green valleys
I try to call to me young ones
but my voice echoes through and through
I love you Utah
You call to my soul
Your azure mountains
Your red cliffs
is a mystery to me
A beauty to me
Ocean
Bring me near to you thundering shore
Were mist flies into the air
Mist is in the air

It has a soothing feeling as it seeps through the door
The seagull's well overhead
Calling for their mate
Their mate calls back to them
A never-ending love song
Sunset, your red and blue hues
Purple and violet
Red and blue
Always calling to you
Sunset
Sunset
You call to me
You give me a feeling
of joy
I sigh as you set
It's night
It's night
Oh how I love the night
You crackle beneath my feet
Your spicy scent sends a thrill
You lift in a quiet breeze
You rustle in the wind
The sky turns orange
As autumn nears
It's chilly
Pumpkins turn
You whisper beneath my feet
As I take long walks
 I hear the wind softly whispering to me
Saying its autumn
Autumn
Autumn
Run
It's chasing after you
I hear its breath behind me as I run
Run
Run
Run
Ah! It's near!
It's catching up to me
I can't help but peek behind me!
I see a face
A face
Hideous to the eyes
It grins at me as I turn sharply away
I shudder!
Get it out!
 Get it out of my head!
He squeals!
I shied away
As we turn a corner
I see a turn in the road
I sigh with relief
But too late
It's got me!
I'm gone!
Gone!
Gone!
Gone!
Gone!
Gone!
Happiness
Happiness
It's a feeling so grand and bold!
I smile as it shoots through me
With ecstasy, It rushes through me
Never wanting to leave my side
But sometimes it has to go

I tell it that sometimes I'll be blue
Even without you
It shrinks,
It frowns,
Can't help but to feel sorry for it
I sigh, you can come in.
Hehe I laugh
A giddy laugh
I let it pulse through me
I smile as I laugh
I laugh
I laugh
Oh, how I laugh!
The giddy feeling never wants to leave
I don't want it to leave
I tell it to stay
It stays.
I can't help but grin
Signing a blissful tune
At my window, I hear a bird sing
With exhaustion and wakefulness
I lay there
Impossible!
With exuberance that seems to fill the room
The sun roles through,
As the sun roles through
Saying hello to the world.
Saying hello to the world
the sun roles through
the room with an exuberance
that seems impossible
I lay there between
Wakefulness
And exhaustion,
I hear a bird signing a blissful tune
At my window
Singing a tune so blissful,
I can't help but grin
At the possibilities that await me!
The rain sings a blissful tune
As he pounds a constant rhythm
 Against my roof
It calms me,
I feel it in my soul,
I feel it in my bones
It's a blissful feeling,
You want to jump up
And dance with all
Your soul,
What a feeling!
I cry my soul is bound
To love you
But you forget,
Forget,
Much to my surprise
You call me by name,
To me you say
To me
The Hen
Or as other people call her
Mother hen
Sits by the window
Staring,
Always staring,
She seems to be
Always staring!
What to do
What to do

Ah move her to the roof
I'll move her to the roof
That way no one will see her
Staring, staring.
The sea
The sea
The sea
Oh how it calls to me
It calls to me
Calls to me
With its thundering surf
It likes to go a Pounding,
It likes to go a Roaring,
It calls to me,
With its endless energy,
It calls to me
Calls to me
Come to me!
Mr. Robin likes to sit in the tree,
He always seems to be singing,
A tune so happy,
It bounces off the roof!
Though with mother hen always staring,
Mr. Robin always seems to be
Distracting me
With that endless staring.
Now Mr. wolf
He is a troublemaker
he loves to sneak around,
with a smirk on his face,
oh! Cries the hen
oh1 cries the Robin
Mr. Wolf is very cunning
He sneaks
And creeps
Always sneaking
And creeping.
Ah me! cries the woman
In the shop
What surprise was written on her face,
Oh, my!
Cries the little old lady
She shakes her head
And wages her head
What a surprise!
Day after day
I see the same person
Giving the same window
The same weird look,
The look of puzzlement,
I have always thought that
It was an act
But the next day I asked him,
He said it was because
He was trying to get rid
Of his shadow,
What nonsense! I say.
The book was always
my morning tradition,
how it made me happy
it could make me scared
or happy
maybe one day I wanted to feel sad
I'd read a sad book
But what use would it be
If I read a sad book
It hard to be said,
I prefer to read books about gusto,

Gusto I say! Is exiting!
Apparently, there is a lone pear
hanging from the tree,
It just floats there,
Lonely, just sitting there.
I have an inner poet,
he sits on my shoulder
and whispers his ideas to me,
some are large and magnificent
and some small and fake,
but nonetheless, he still whispers to me.
You like to sit on my shoulders
 and keep me warm,
like a little old granny, you sit there
looking down on us with your caring stare,
you wrap yourself around me
always keeping me warm,
though the negative part
are you blind me when I look up at you
as much as I love you,
you blind me with your pale yellow glow.
It doesn't matter if you come,
On time
Or late
You always get there,
It is a mystery opening you,
I never know what's inside
Then when I do open it not be such a surprise.
Surprise! yell the family
I fall over with surprise
 and they gather around me,
what?
What?
Do they cry
I smile and say
Nothing at all.
It's late
Late!
Late!
What shall I do?
I scurry around
Trying to get all done
But no use I am late.
She stands there watching me
With her brunet hair
She swishes it back and forth
Trying to get my attention,
She tries to make eye contact with me,
But no use,
But I'm oblivious to her
I stare at another goes by
I am entranced.
 He wrestles to and fro
Trying to gain ground
The opponent throws him under
He groans
Can't win,
Can't give up, can't give up!
The sleeper
She sleeps peacefully
As I watch her,
She seems so calm
When she's asleep,
She doesn't yell at me
It's a relief!
food will sustain you
but to have it sustain you
you need to eat,

bacon, sizzling on the grill,
its smell makes my mouth water
my little brother is looking up at me with pleading eyes,
it smells so good, he whispers,
eggs cooking in the pan,
sizzling in the heat,
next, comes the dog he whimpers trying to get your attention,
you look down and see him with pleading eyes,
saying please feed me!
you see the eggs turning from white to yellow,
yellow like rays of sunshine,
again you mouth waters at the
overcoming a sense of smell that's
overloading my nose,
I take a deep breath in and smile,
Egg and bacon is a wonderful sense of smell.
Fruit it has a bounty of taste,
One moment it's sweet,
The next it is so juicy,
The juice runs down your chin
In rivulets,
Your stomach growls with pleasure.
wind rushing through the trees,
it rushes,
depending on the year it blows,
blows with a happy purpose spreading the flowers,
freshening the air,
when it's summer,
it blows through the clouds,
scattering them like sheep.
Swinging around and around,
Around you go,
Smiling at the gleeful feeling that fills you,
You jump, you soar,
Stamp your feet little one,
Dance, dance around the tree,
Little one go far,
Go far.
Music inspires me,
It brings images and words to mind,
When it comes I write,
And write well,
Says teachers,
I scratch and scratch again,
On the pad,
write and write I do,
Fast as light,
I do write.

The fiery dance,
Spinning out of control,
You spin,
An endless weight,
Spin and spin,
Jump, leap,
Through the air, you leap,
Fluid motions guide you,
Tap your toes,
Fly through air,
You are weightless,
Spinning through the air,
Spinning out of control,
You feel free,
You come to a slow descent,
You stop.
Over mountains, you climb,
The pines are aflame,
On the high,

The winds were rushing,
The flame was red,
It spreads,
High into the mountains you go,
Whistling a nameless tune,
You climb,
Over the mount, you climb,
To see flame,
You sag with grief,
All the hard work,
You put in,
You finally see two shapes walking through the flame.
The wings of the angel beat,
Beat,
Beat,
With a constant rhythm,
You fly through the air,
Rising higher,
And higher,
You rise,
Glorious of heaven.
By blackened beak
And by blackened bone,
The night watchers crawl,
Crawl to one of bone,
And one of stone,
Hark! Hark! They cry,
To the blue corn moon,
To the wild midnight moon,
The man in the moon,
Crawls down from the moon,
To the heartless woman in the dune,
They glare and glare,
They hiss and hiss,
But compared to bliss,
They are not of this boon.
The cry goes up and down
Down and up
Screeching and wailing
Wailing and screeching
It never stops
The child cries and cries
Such a harsh sound
It's hard to the ears
Unceasing,
My head spines
My world rocks back and forth
With the unceasing sound
Of the babies cry.
It's impeccable!
They came to my house
And cried happy birthday,
The day was a succession of surprises.
The old man sits in a corner and laments
Sits for three weeks
Lamenting,
Always lamenting
Always mourning,
He grumps in the corner,
He grumps in the street
He grumps
He grumps,
He laments
He laments
Over and over again.
The buffoon climbs around the pole
Making people roll their eyes
Making them laugh at his stupidity,

The buffoon is a buffoon always,
He could make me laugh
Or he could make me roll my eyes in annoyance.
Happy
Happy day
I laugh the day is so warm
The flowers are blooming
Pocking through the dirt
Little flowers shinning their faces
through the dirt smiling at the sky.
Pale moon, shining, shine among the fair people,
sighing with content they glide across the moonlight shore.
Their feet hardly touch the water that they glide along.
Fair hair shines pale silver in the moonlight.
Their faces caught up in ecstasy shine up to the sky.
Their faces glimmer happiness pure. Pure as gold.
Golden light drifts from their beings as they glide along.
The golden light is a cloak shining behind them.
By fair moonlight, they glide. Glide from land to land.
By fair moonlight, they do a good deed.
None other than they may see themselves above the moon and the stars.
Above the moon and stars shine the slight star they call Edorras.
Edorras shines brightly giving hope in slight times.
Their land Lightlee shines below them in pale slumber.
Slumber so thick it's mistaken for water.
Children quietly sing hymns to their elders as they pass away.
Passing to another world beyond their sight.
Their hymns are softly floating through the air.
The air shivers with the beauty of it.
Their song is a hymn to the world.
Making it beautiful again.


Pale slumber awaits the soul.
Awaking dreams flit to the forefront of my mind.
Brief flashes of sleepy colors cross the mind as we fall slowly into our waking dreams.
Peace, warmth and drowsiness fill your mind.
Sleep is just another journey to a different but beautiful world.
A world at its edges are gray.
With brief flash of pale gold.
And in the midst of the world a hazy dream like state that fills the mind.
Filling it with fantasies never before seen.
Dancers flit from one scene to the next.
Flowing like water through the air.
Your dreams become a dance performance.
People gliding by on light feet.
Their faces filled with joy at the thought of being able to fly through the air without a thought.


Eyes flutter like butterflies,
fighting the sleep overtaking the body.
Dark corners of the mind speak silence
as clouds of unintelligible scenes dance in the spotlight.
Colors and words,
Colors and words,
that's all it is but dreams pull it into a galaxy of a story.
Characters pulled from the day's play and toil.


And then a fantastic play starts.
A hero sings from a tree above.
 A young madden glides up the hill towards him.
A tall knight in shining armor.

And now to the next scene.
As beautiful as the first.
A young child running across a prairie.
A smile crossing her face.
Golden hair flies from her back.
She is running so fast that her hair becomes wind and then she too becomes wind.
 A giddy laugh fills the air as she starts to sour into the air.
A white Horse follows the girl of wind and they join together becoming faster than before.
They are free.
A flash of silver and gold light flying through the air.
And every time the horse and the child passes you can hear the child laughing with joy.
And the horse calling to the wind.


Seconds later the wind turns cold sending shivers down your spine,
you don black clothes layering against the fierce wind and mourn the absence of sweet Persephone.
You smile for she's with her love and trudge on wishing them well.


And then sleep falls heavy and thick as the mortal soul falls into a pale slumber.
Waking dreams await the mind.
As you fall asleep you see flashes of gold and silver.
Dreams so life like it's all the same.


Color and words,
color and words,
that's all it is,
you welcome it with open arms,
and warm blankets.


Sleep warm and well my dear child for night is upon us.
May good fortune watch us as we sleep.
And Mother Nature watch over us.
Pale slumber awaits you my dear child.
Golden flashes of light flit through the mind my dear child.
Sleep in a pale slumber in trees of green.
Golden light filtering through the leaves.
Sleep, sleep my child. All is well, all is well.
Your father watches over you with a loving eye.
Sleep my child sleep.
Fall into easy sleep as I watch over you.
Edoras fair sings fair music above the forest green.

Made in the USA
Monee, IL
26 June 2025

20051301R10031